Three Bullets

Other books by Melvin Burgess

An Angel for May
The Baby and Fly Pie
Bloodsong
Bloodtide
Burning Issy
The Cry of the Wolf
Doing It
Junk
Lady: My Life as a Bitch
The Lost Witch
Nicholas Dane
Sara's Face

MELVIN BURGESS

ANDERSEN PRESS

First published in 2021 by
Andersen Press Limited
20 Vauxhall Bridge Road
London SW1V 2SA
Vijverlaan 48, 3062 HL Rotterdam, Nederland
www.andersenpress.co.uk

2 4 6 8 10 9 7 5 3 1

British Library Cataloguing in Publication Data available.

ISBN 978 1 83913 050 2

Printed and bound in Great Britain
by Clays Ltd, Elcograf S.p.A.

Ruled Britannia

This book is part of a triptych of novels; three separate stories all taking place in the same imagined world. *One Drop*, by Pete Kalu, *The Second Coming*, by Tariq Mehmood, as well as my own book, *Three Bullets*, all take place in the UK as it might be in the near future.

Thanks to Pete and Tariq not just in terms of world building but with conversations about race, politics, gender and life in general, not to mention all the hard work that went into writing notes for one another. You guys opened a lot of doors for me – I've not had so much fun writing a book for years.

You can find out more about the Triptych on our Facebook page, https://www.facebook.com/RuledBritannia/
Or at www.ruledbritannia.net

For my Anita,
who made Lockdown such a pleasure

1

My name is Martina. You won't like me, not many people do. Back then I lived in south Manchester with my little brother Rowan, an odious brat; my mum, a nutjob; and my friend Maude, who I used to hate but, well, she didn't turn out as bad as she might have done, put it like that. She kind of owed me, which helped. If it wasn't for me, she'd have been dead meat by then, no question.

Not so long before, I had loads of friends – well, people I knew, anyway. Not all of them were exactly friends. Now I just had Maude. She used to go to the same school as me, back in the day. We never hung out. She was way over my head. She was two years older than me and she was everything I'm not. She was *hot*. I'm not hot. Mind you, she didn't stay so hot, not without the hot short skirts and the hot tight jeans and the hot make-up. She still had the nice bum and boobs but if you dropped her back in a half decent school, she would truly *not* be lead bitch. She still got loads of boys but all you needed round there to get any number of boys was a pair of legs you could still open and that was as good as hot.

She was smart as well, which I never was – I mean, good-at-lessons smart. Good at sport and that. Oh, and a bitch. Did I mention that? A bully. You know the sort. She wouldn't even

1

talk to me because I wasn't cool enough. She was in a group of girls who somehow found out that I was wearing a thong one day and pulled my skirt up over my head so that everyone could see my spotty bottom. That was nice.

Then her house got bombed, and her mum and dad both got killed, and her brother, who she adored, pulled her out of the rubble, put her on a mattress on the side of the road and ran away to who-knows-where.

Maude's brother did the sensible thing. If my mum had been as dead as hers, I'd have gone, too. I'd've gone before you could lick the fat off your fingers. I was furious when my dad dragged her home on that mattress to live with us. I never saw a lot of my dad because he was always away doing important war stuff. So then what? He finally gets home after being away for months, and the first thing he does is adopt the monster bitch girl from school who spent three months calling me Cheesewire. And then he goes away again! How's that for fair, eh, Dad?

'I don't care how horrible she was, she has nothing now,' he said. Then he left us again to get on with his war work.

See? Mum needed him. I needed him. *We* needed him. And instead of helping us, he spent all his time helping everyone else. Then he brings in cheesewire girl and leaves us on our own to look after *her*!

Unbelievable.

I remember standing in the doorway of her room, looking at her lying there, all bruised and ugly. One side of her face was out like a melon, she had a bloodstained bandage around her head. She'd been bleeding from her ear.

'Not so hot now, are you?' I said.

I said it quite loud. Loud enough for her to hear if she was awake – if she could still hear – but not loud enough for Mum to hear downstairs. She opened her eyes, looked at me, turned over and lay still.

Serves you right, I thought. But I felt bad.

She woke up a few days later and I still don't know if she heard me that day. But I really hope not because we became mates. She spent a week eating all the Pot Noodles I'd got from when they bombed the Co-op, then one day she lifted her head and looked at me across the table.

'Did you get them?' she asked. 'The noodles?'

I nodded. She nodded.

'I'm sorry,' she said. 'I'm really, really sorry, Marti.' I suppose she was talking about the thong and stuff. 'I'll come out with you tomorrow and help.'

And she did. And – she was OK, Maude. She stuck to her word, for you or against you, which I liked. She had principles, which I kind of admired because I don't have any myself.

'A person who stands for nothing will fall for anything,' she kept telling me. Which was really annoying because I lent her that book, and also because she's the one who fell for people's bullshit every time. All you had to do was agree with her and she'd follow you anywhere. I called her Rubblehead because I think all that rubble sitting on her head for a day must have knocked some generosity of spirit into her.

'You were such a bitch before. That bomb was a blessing,' I told her. And she laughed, but actually it's true. See? Even bombs can be a blessing.

That was a joke. Right?

2

So I woke up and it was pitch black, and I couldn't see a thing and there was a great bellowing and roaring all around.

I thought, This is it. There was a big crash and a bang that knocked the breath out of me. There were bombs going off all around. It was pitch black but then there was this blinding white flash for a moment, and everything looked normal. The room, everything. I was still in bed. The walls, still there. I saw it all in a fraction of a second. The door. The glass was still in the windows, but this weird blanket of dust was creeping in at the edges.

My mum was always nagging us to sleep down in the basement with her and Rowan, but I had my reasons for staying on the first floor. There's lots of ways to die when your house gets hit. You can get burned to death. You can have a lump of masonry fall on your head. You can choke on smoke or get thrown up into the air and come down on the heap of rubble that was once your bedroom. Or, you can get buried under the wreckage with slow internal bleeding that hurts like hell, with not enough air to breathe and tonnes of bricks pressing down on top of you, hoping someone will come along and dig you out but knowing that they probably won't. I'd put some thought into this and that last one was my least favourite way of dying. Which is why I always slept on the first floor. The attic – even a little bomb is going to come through the roof and get you. Ground floor, if the house falls down – you're dead.

Technically the basement was the safest place, but that basement was so cold and damp. The gas went last year and we only got electric for a few hours here and there.

I got this horrendous vertigo, like I was falling, but I was still in the room lying on my bed. Then, a big bump. The glass shattered in the windows. The incendiaries were flashing – one, two, three, four, like that – and I could see Maude sitting up in bed with her hair in little curls sticking up. She turned to look at me in strobe and I remember it so well, her with her blonde hair all sticking up with all that gel she used, like some crazy doll. I just had time to notice that there was something funny about the ceiling when the room began to fill up with dust. Thicker and thicker. Suddenly we were both choking and we knew we had to get out quick.

I jumped up and my head hit the roof. The room had shrunk! I was like, WTF? but there was no time to think. There was another flash and you could see how the dust was swirling around by the broken windows. I bent down under my bed to drag out my backpack, but the space under the bed had shrunk just like the room had and it was jammed tight.

'Marti!' Maude shrieked, because I wasn't getting out fast enough. You could hear the whole house groaning. But no way, *no way* was my beloved backpack staying behind because then I might just as well be dead. So I was up on my feet and heaving and tugging at it, screaming, 'Maude, Maude!' as loud as I could for her to help me, and we were both coughing and hacking and choking. But then there was another flash and that

5

damn ceiling was even lower, like it was some kind of monster psycho ceiling coming to get me, with cracks all over it and its insides spilling out through them, so I had to leave the backpack after all and make a dash for the window. There was both of us scrambling out, getting cut on the jags of broken glass still in the window. I cut myself badly, actually, on the arm and on my thigh. It was the dead of night. So dark. There was another flash – thank God! You have no idea how dark it gets when there's no electricity. But that dust – you couldn't even breathe. Claustrophobia? Tell me about it.

We got out onto the flat bit on top of the bay window and scuttled to the edge and then paused. It was a big drop from up there. Bombs were still going off nearby and we were still getting flashes of lights from incendiaries – but Lo! The whole house had shrunk. Instead of a view across to the stumps of the university buildings on the other side of Platt Fields, we were halfway to the ground.

What must have happened, we worked out later, is bombs must have gone off on each side of the house. The blast punched in the ground-floor walls so the house folded up under us like a pack of cards, and the attic floor above us, which was a rubbish floor that a cheap builder put in for Mum and Dad when I was just a wean, came down inside our room more or less in one piece, which is why the ceiling was so close.

We were both hanging on for dear life because it was a long way down from there normally, but when the next burst of incendiaries went off, you could see that actually, now it was just a short drop down. So we just stepped down from the top of the bay window, which should have been three metres off the ground, straight into the front garden.

We stood there a moment coughing, like, *Really? Is that it?* We couldn't believe we were out, just like that. We walked together across the road like a couple of old folk going for a stroll and looked back to where the house was, which was like a ghost house, in complete and utter darkness, except for the flashes, which were getting duller now as the incendiaries marched past us. The whole thing was totally surreal.

'So I was right about sleeping up there,' I said.

'Yeah,' said Maude. 'Unbelievable. I mean, it looks like that was the only floor that was . . .'

I knew what she was about to say. The first floor was the only one you stood a decent chance of coming out of alive. But then we both looked at each other, because in our relief at being alive, we forgot . . .

Maude said '—Mum.'

She'd started to call my mum just Mum, which annoyed me because she was *my* mum, not hers. But I didn't pick her up on it because – yeah, Mum! She was under all that rubble.

'Rowan,' she said.

'My backpack,' I said, and we both ran back to the house just in time to see it go up. There was no warning – no missile or whistle or anything. It just went *boom*. We both flew up in the air in the blast. I didn't actually see it because I was going backwards at the time. Then I was rolling around on my back with bits of brick and smoking sparks falling around me, trying to get my breath and work out how many ribs I'd broken. None actually, thanks for asking. By the time I got to sit up, everything was in darkness again and you could just hear this rumbling, crashing, rolling kind of noise, which I think must have been the house falling down. Jesus. Later, I always thought of that as the sound of my mum dying.

We ran up to it, but bits of house were still falling off and it was too dangerous. It was dark, there was fire inside the house but you couldn't see much. You could *hear* stuff hitting the ground around you. It was hard to breathe. It started raining. I remember being surprised at how cold the rain was. Quite icy on the skin. It's funny what stays in your head. We stood at the front where her bedroom used to be, shouting, 'Mum! Mum! Mum!' at the top of our voices at the heaps of bricks, but no one answered. The bombs were still marching about but further away now.

People came out with torches and shovels and stuff to help. Once the dust began to clear – the rain helped – you could see the house was just a pile of rubble and tangled beams and windows and cables and pipes and bits of fire and things. Our things. We pulled away at it all night, and it was the hardest and most horrible work anyone ever did. We didn't get any sleep, obvs. When the morning came and we could see, the devastation was so bad, you just knew you were wasting your time. Some of the neighbours drifted off, but we didn't stop. We took breaks from the digging at Thomas's house across the road, sipping hot tea and eating chickpeas with the other casualties. Veronica from next door had lost her house too. It actually looked as if it had fallen sideways onto ours, which irritated me. I mean – it just made things worse, you know?

She bandaged up my thigh for me. No one cried. What can you do? You just sit there and think to yourself that one day, maybe soon, you're going to cry your eyes out about this. But not now.

3

Mum and my brother Rowan had been sleeping in the basement which had the two side walls fall in on it and the ceiling, our floor, came down on top of that. So they were dead, weren't they? Flat as cereal packets. Even so, I dug for two days to get down to them, then at the end of the second day, when we reached ground zero – Mum zero, let's face it – that's when I got the willies and Maude and some of the neighbours made me go and wait across the road while they cleared off the final layers. It took them a few hours until Maude came to find me and gave me a little nod, and I didn't follow her when she went back. I didn't want to see it, thanks.

I cried then. Then, I cried. She'd been a crap mum for the last couple of years, but that was just because she couldn't cope with the war and the bombs and the people dying so she got into all this weird secrecy and hiding and conspiracy theories. But before that, she'd been a good mum. And even if she hadn't been, she was still *my* mum, the only mum I'd ever had or could have, and you have to love your mum, don't you? – the woman who gave birth to you and loved you no matter what.

We buried her a couple of days later in the Central Cemetery. I'm mostly glad I never got to see her dead, because who knows what she was like underneath all that rubble? In another way, though, it does my head in because I keep getting these fantasies, like the one where she's just popped out to see someone so she wasn't even in when the house got hit, or perhaps she was having a secret affair with someone, but she got stuck and only came back after we left, and now she's looking everywhere for us and can't find us. Whereas, if I'd seen her, in whatever mess she was in, then I'd know for sure she was dead, right here in my heart, and that she is never going to come back.

But whatever my heart thought and hoped, my brain knew. My mum was dead and I was an orphan, free to realise my dream of running away from this benighted s***hole and make my home somewhere decent, somewhere with shops and beauty spas and schools and hospitals that don't get bombed. The good things in life. I remembered them and I wanted them back. Hot chocolate and tea. Nice meals every day, cake, going to the cinema, make-up, eating out, pizza, burgers, frothy coffee. Wine. Vodka. Sex. Drugs. All of it.

I know what you're thinking. You're thinking, What a monster! Her mum's just been squashed flat like a beetle and here she is celebrating her freedom. But don't get me wrong – I loved my mum. Not my brother Rowan, though. I didn't love him, that's true, so in that respect I *am* a monster. But my mum, yeah. Every time I think about her, even now, it hurts like a punch to the stomach. She was such a stubborn bitch! And a stupid cow, as I often had to remind her. I didn't *like* her much, but I loved her and I wept my little heart out, all on my own, sitting on the loo in Thomas's basement, until someone knocked on the door and said they needed a poo, so I wiped my eyes on some toilet paper and got on with life.

There was only one thing for me to do now. Get the you-know-what out of there and start to *live*.

We'd had to dig down through our room to get down to Mum, so I'd already pulled out some of my stuff. A few clothes. I got my board that I painted in art class while school was still going: 'Who is Martina Okoro?' Some other bits and pieces. Couple of books. My Black Sabrina doll with the braids and hair extensions. I used to collect them for a while until I got sick of how pretty they all were – they were making me jealous – so I got rid of them all except her. My money I'd saved. Yeah, and a little bag with some gold in it. A gold chain, a few gold coins. My secret phone, which was still there under the mattress where I hid it when I slept. But most importantly – I got my backpack! Yeah! My backpack had been packed for years, just waiting for the chance to get out of this dump to a sensible country where you can actually have a life.

It was time to go. I'd spent the past few years hanging around against my better judgment looking after my mum. It was time to think about myself for a change. We all have our dreams and ambitions. Some want to Do Good, some want to travel, some want to make loads of money. I wanted to spend my war being decadent. Drugs, booze and sex. Mostly sex. Lots of sex. Every single way you can imagine.

People who know me would be surprised to hear me say that because I'm such a prude. I *never* swear. I can't watch when a sex scene comes on a film, I have to put my head in my hands or look the other way. I'm such an iron virgin that not only have I never had sex, I've never even been *kissed*. It's true. But inside, there's a dirty bitch waiting to come out who only I know, just waiting for the right chance to be introduced to the right people. It's just that none of them have chanced along to meet me yet.

I was soooo looking forward to it.

I was already packed – I'd been packing for years. That backpack was the first thing I went looking for after the bomb, because you can bet there were plenty of people beetling about in the rubble that day, pretending to help, who were really just looking out for what they could loot. I can't tell you how relieved I was to get to it first, still intact.

All the essentials were in there. Underwear. Five or six changes of clothes. Make-up. Books – *The Gender Games* and my copy of the autobiography of Malcolm X, that my dad gave to me. If I wasn't so besotted with Beyoncé, it would be Malcolm X who'd be my hero. His motto is my motto: 'By any means necessary'. It's just that he wanted equal rights by any means necessary, and I want to get out of this hole and get stoned and you-know-whated by any means necessary. I know a lot of people who admire Malcolm X as much as I do, but none of them admire him quite like me. The big difference is that whereas they admire him for the Black liberation years, I revere him for the New York years, when he was out there busy getting his hair straightened into a conk, taking loads of cocaine, wearing a zoot and sleeping with white girls.

And my meds, they were in there. About three months'

supply – enough to get me to Amsterdam, city of fun, where you can buy the things over the counter, so they say. I'm never without a supply of meds. You better believe it.

I have family in Amsterdam. One, maybe two half brothers from my dad's past life. I haven't heard from them in ages and I've never seen much of them anyway so I can't say that they're the main attraction. But it helps to have a foothold, you know what I mean?

Once I left the loo, I got outside, hid myself away round behind the back of Thomas's house and took out my secret phone and my earphones to listen to some tunes. The phone had a bit of juice in it, where I'd charged it at Thomas's generator. Nothing but the best for our Thomas.

It was one of my very precious things, that phone. It was a present from my dad, the last present he ever gave me before he disappeared. He left one with Maude and one with Mum, but would you believe those bitches, they lost theirs ages ago, which was really careless of them, because they both knew how important the software on it was to Dad and the people he worked with. Not to mention all those poor suckers down there in the ERAC at Huntingdon, who were having their brains spring-cleaned twice a day, courtesy of the Brotherhood of the Blood of Jesus. You want to know how important that software actually was? So important it had been bugged so that it couldn't be copied, or downloaded or duplicated in case anyone fiddled with it or put a virus in it or learned how to decode it. That important. Yes, those bitches had lost their phones and I still had mine, like the faithful daughter I was.

Which meant I had the only copy of Dad's Very Important Software existing on the entire planet. Big responsibility, huh?

Who'd have thought it?

You might not have heard about the ERAC at Huntingdon. The Bloods never exactly advertised it, obvs, and our lot up here, the FNA, the Free Northern Army, they were never too keen on making it public knowledge either. It's the old story. Most of them refused to believe it existed in the first place, and the ones that did were like, Are you kidding? You want *us* to deal with something happening way down there? That's up to the East Anglian bunch, or the southern bunch. We're too busy fighting for our own people.

ERAC stands for Evangelical Realignment Centre. It's where the Bloods fix up idolaters and heretics and believers in equal rights, that sort of thing, to put them back on the straight and narrow. Of course, being white supremacists, they have their own ways of working out if you are a heretic. So for instance, if you're south Asian in descent, you're a Muslim. Stands to reason. If you're Black, you may or may not be a Muslim, but best to take no chances. If you're a Black Christian, you're going to be the wrong kind of Christian, and if you're not a Christian, you'll have more than likely got your head full of all that equal rights nonsense anyway. Best to shove you in there, too.

I'm not saying there's no white people in ERAC, just that

they need pretty good proof that you belong there. As opposed to no proof whatsoever if you're Black.

White supremacists, don't cha just love 'em?

The ERAC isn't just any old internment camp. It's an experimental facility. They put a chip in your head, an actual microchip, and they reboot your identity with it. I know! Don't ask. It literally makes my skin crawl. They use some kind of software, but software just happens to be the thing my dad was a genius at. He'd been developing a virus that could undo the damage.

Clever stuff. Clever Dad. And he may have actually done it, too. He was just about to go down south to deliver the software when he vanished overnight. Fortunately he'd put copies of it on these phones which he then handed out – one to Mum, one to me and one to Maude – to keep safe if anything happened to him.

. . . Not that there was any need to say anything about me still having that phone to Maude. She didn't need to know everything. I told myself, 'It's a safe bet that if she does ever find out I still have it, she will seriously try to kill me.' As far as she was concerned my phone disappeared in the same police raid as hers and Mum's a few days after Dad disappeared. We thought we were safe from the Bloods because at that time, they were a hundred miles away still busy fighting for Birmingham. It must have been a task force they sent up from down there, just to take my dad out. They knew what a genius he was, even if the FNA didn't. They took him out and I guess we ought to be thankful they didn't come back and take us out as well. But they didn't. Instead they came back and took all the hardware we had – laptops, phones, USB

16

sticks, the lot. My dad's software, that he had spent his life working on – gone. Every last copy. And yet . . . here was my phone that Dad gave me, right here in my hand. Odd, eh? The world is full of contradictions, isn't it? You just never can tell.

I only kept it because it was a real good phone, better than my other one. It had my music on it, including the playlist my dad made for me. Wi-fi was on and off like a traffic light, the mobile masts were always being knocked out, so if you wanted tunes on demand, you needed a hard copy. Normally I kept the secret phone, well . . . secret. You know? And quiet. But on this occasion my other phone, my cheap, nasty public phone, didn't make it out of the house, so there was no choice if I wanted to listen to my tunes. Even so, I *so* wished I didn't have it, because what it meant was, that before heading off to Hull to catch a ferry on my way to Amsterdam, city of my dreams and my future home, I was supposed to go south, down towards Blood territory to deliver the software and fulfil my dad's crazy dreams of giving all those poor lost souls in the ERAC their freedom. Who, frankly, were never any of my business in the first place, except that he made me promise I would.

Except – really? I mean – *really?* Yes, I know I promised my dad if anything happened to him I'd make sure that software got down to the ERAC in Huntingdon. And yes, I know that Maude's poor heart had been broken into a thousand pieces when all that hardware went missing, taking my dad's dreams with them, which of course had become her dreams too, ever since he saved her life . . . But the thing is this; no one in the world – *no one* – had any idea that I still had that phone with my dad's software intact. And . . .

Dad was dead, wasn't he? He *had* to be dead – why would the Bloods keep someone like him alive? And promises don't count to dead people, do they? My dad was a man with a huge brain, so huge that when he spoke to you, you often didn't know what he was talking about. Tell the truth, I sometimes wonder if he understood himself. Yeah, he was a brain. But he was a dead brain now.

I kneeled down there among the bins, where I doubtless belonged. The sweet notes of Sylvester's 'You Make Me Feel (Mighty Real)' filled my ears. A message from my dad. I tapped my fingers on my knee in time to the music. I could hear my dad in my ear, saying . . . 'Is it a man? Is it a woman? Do we care? NOOOOOOO!'

When we first realised that Dad had gone from our lives for ever, first thing Maude did was try to give the software to the FNA. But as far as they were concerned, my dad was just another crazy old Black man with a bunch of crazy old Black dreams that were never going to come true. After that, when they said no, she was all ready to set off on her own, all the way down there, into the very teeth of the enemy, to deliver a phone full of crazy software to some guy my dad used to know, who might not even be alive any more. Even though she'd almost certainly never make it. Even though she had no idea whether the software would even work or not. And even though she really owed it to me to stay and help me look after my mum, because I was the one who saved her life.

But! Guess what? It came to pass that it was exactly at that moment that the Bloods came and raided our house, so she couldn't go and had to stay and help me look after Mum after all.

So there I was behind the bins, thinking, Hmmm. So, what's it gonna be, Marti? Amsterdam, with its drugs, sex and its cheap, hedonistic lifestyle? Or the ERAC, with the Bloods and all their attendant oppression, racism, torture, rape and almost certain death? Because, let's face it, as I stood there in my stockinged feet, I represented everything – *everything* – that the Bloods hated. If they ever got their hands on me, I was worse than dead. They'd spend the rest of eternity beating me up and pulling out my fingernails just for fun.

Now let me see . . .

In case you're wondering, I'm not a Muslim. Neither was my mum or my dad. And I'm not a Christian or political or anything really, except I'm really, really, really pro-Martina Okoro. So what is it about me they would hate so much?

You may well ask.

The music moved on. It was my hero, Beyoncé. I love her so much. I want to be as much like her as it's possible to be. Same face, same boobs, same life. I know, I know! Dream on. But we all need an ambition in life to keep us going. Mine just happens to be being Beyoncé.

I sat there for a few more minutes, waiting and thinking, thinking and waiting. What was it to be? Fulfilling my dad's noble ambitions – or my petty, small selfish ones? Putting myself in grave personal danger for the greater good, or running for cover and a selfish, hedonistic lifestyle? Fighting for hope, freedom and democracy for my fellow countrymen – or making a run for it to grab whatever I could for myself?

No competition, was it?

Sorry, Dad. I know how much you wanted to help mankind, but the present is more important than the future. More to the point – I am more important than them.

And you? You're dead.

I got up. I had things to do. On the way out I walked right past the bins – Thomas still kept his bins, the snob, even though no one had collected any rubbish for years – but I didn't throw the phone away. Not yet. Those tunes were a present from my dad. They were like messages – memories, bits of information, beliefs. In a way, they were all I had of him.

I loved my dad at least as much as I loved my mum, maybe even more. I don't think I liked him much more than her, but I *admired* him. My mum was too fragile for this world. She didn't have it in her. Actually, I think Mum would have had a hard time coping even in the land of milk and honey, let alone the land of shrapnel and bullet wounds. But my dad was brave and clever and determined – all the things that I'm not and never will be. He seemed to really believe that he could force the world to see things the way he did – which was nonsense of course, but you have to admire him for it. He picked those tunes for me. It was stuff he liked, stuff I'd liked at various times of my life. Stuff my mum liked. Songs that he wanted me to know about, or that showed me something he thought was important. He'd really thought about it, like he thought about everything. He was dead, dead as a leg of lamb. He was a lousy dad even when he was alive, always away looking after anyone on Earth so long as they weren't related to him, as far as I could make out. But those songs were all I had of him, and I wasn't anywhere near ready to chuck them in the bin.

4

While I was busy planning our escape, Maude was still at it, pulling, digging, chopping her way through the beams. She kept saying she could hear something under there, voices, bangs and so on, but it was obviously just the house settling. A bomb goes off, *BANG,* and your house falls down, but it spends a while settling. Bits fall off. It creaks and groans and sometimes – often – it sounds like voices. But it isn't voices, except once in a hundred. It's two beams rubbing themselves together, or the last bit of breath being squeezed out of your mum's cold dead body, most likely. No one gets out after three days under the rubble. After two days, if they do find you, you probably wish they hadn't. It wound me up, to be honest. I was on at her to pack it in. She was going to need that energy for later on.

'We can't leave until we're sure,' she kept saying. And I was like, What are you going to do, move the whole house with your bare hands?

'If I have to,' she said.

See? I don't call her Rubblehead for nothing. She got a thing in her head, that's it, for weeks. She used to be such a cow, then she tried to make up for it by being a saint. And she had no sense of self-preservation. Which is fine, but she'd not only give *her* last crust of bread to some poor old woman who's going to die anyway – honestly, I've seen her do it – she'd give *my* last crust of bread to some poor old woman who's going to die anyway. Which is unacceptable. It's a war zone, Maude! You don't *do* that sort of thing. You look after yourself. There's no shame in it. You have to.

The situation was getting urgent; the Muslims were arriving. I saw some in Withington when I went out to see what was going on. At that point it was just a few dozen, hanging out on the pavements, little groups of them, trying to catch my eye and give me the nod, working out if I was one of them or not. Well, I wasn't. I didn't nod back, I kept my eyes straight. I didn't have anything I wanted to share with them.

They weren't getting what you'd call a warm welcome. It wasn't like we had enough ourselves. With all those extra mouths to feed, things were going to get a lot worse pretty quickly. The ones I saw in Withington were just the start. We'd all seen the tanks rolling into Birmingham, seen the columns of refugees on our screens – miles and miles of them, strung out along the M6, marching north, overwhelming towns and villages on the way. Tens of thousands of them, maybe hundreds of thousands, marching up the country because they'd been pushed out of their homes by the regime. That had been going on ever since the US put the Bloods in charge after the war down south a couple of years ago. They'd chased the Muslims out of London first, so they'd all gone to Birmingham. Now the Bloods had taken Birmingham so they were all coming up here. You see? Once us brownskins started arriving in Manchester in numbers, you can bet the regime would be right behind them.

Manchester was going right down the pan and it was going to

get worse, fast. As soon as the Bloods got here, we were going down. There was no unity. The Free Northern Army controlled the south of the city, the fascists had the north, the east was in bits, that sort of thing. There were snipers and street-to-street fighting, all that. There was shelling and bombs going off, it had been going on for three years or more already, ever since the government fell and the civil war got going properly. Things had got a lot worse in the past six months or so with the real heavy bombing, the air raids, when the Bloods began advancing north. Softening us up, I suppose. It wasn't just them, either. The big powers never want to risk their own boys on the ground, so they help their chosen side with bombs. Don't ask me who it was dropped that junk on us in Fallowfield, there's so many different sides, I can't even count that high. Probably the US, who hated the FNA. Turkey may have had a few planes going over. The Gulf, Europe. I don't know. The point is the Muslims and the Blacks, the commies and the queers and the libertarians, etc were all coming and the Bloods were behind them and when they came, they'd bring along the big stuff – American stuff. Tanks, heavy artillery, helicopter gunships. And troops. Lots of troops. Lots of heavily armed troops. We were not going to be on the payroll. Maybe they were a few months away, maybe a few weeks, maybe even a few days. But they were coming, and by the time they got here, I wanted to be gone. I wanted to be gone yesterday.

I ran back home to tell Maude it was time to stop digging.

Thomas, our neighbour who'd taken us in, he had this big old house, the biggest on our road and it hadn't been touched.

Even his croquet lawn at the back was still in one piece, which was ridiculous really, because we'd all sorts of stuff going off all over Fallowfield lately. It was just him and his mum living there so he had loads of room and he was very good after the bombings. He opened up his basement for people – had a family of six living down there who'd been bombed out a few weeks before. He was very generous but he was hilarious too – he used to go down there with an air freshener and spray all over them and bellow at them in that big operatic voice of his about personal hygiene.

'The waft comes up every time I open the cellar door,' he bellowed. It wasn't their fault, there wasn't enough water for all those people to shower every day like he did. Also, Thomas had somehow got his hands on half a dozen sacks of chickpeas, don't ask me where from, I don't know. He knew so many people, he was always coming up with something. We'd all been eating nothing else for two days, so everyone was farting away like Queen Elizabeth II after a heavy week of banqueting. It was a miasma down there! You could spray all you liked and never get rid of that honk.

But not us. Maude and I were from across the road. We were neighbours. I used to go to parties at his house when I was little with Mum and Dad and play croquet. He used to let me have a sip of fizz while they weren't looking.

'I'm not having you staying down with the riff-raff,' he said. 'You get the posh treatment. You're guests.' So we had one of the spare bedrooms on the top floor.

He was a singing teacher – opera. There was always someone round there yodelling away in one of those big opera voices,

25

even during all that chaos. There was one there when I arrived. A girl. Very beautiful and very surreal, that beautiful voice soaring over the rubble of our house as I came up the road. I went in the back way, past his mother Lily, sitting watching soaps he'd recorded for her years ago at high volume in the conservatory.

'Marti, darling, how nice to see you, make me a cup of tea, will you?' she warbled as I ran past. But I was in a hurry. I ran up the stairs two at a time. We had to GO!

I burst into our room and guess what? Guess bloody what? She'd found someone under the rubble after all. There he was on the bed – *our* bed – with a drip going into his cute little arm and an oxygen mask over his cute little face.

You guessed it. It was Rowan. She'd only dug out Rowan. The surviving little . . . survivor.

'You found *him*?' I said. 'Of all the things you could have found – him? *Him*, Maude?'

'He was under the stairwell,' she said, which made sense because Mum was always on at us to hide in the stairwell, or in the fireplace. They were the two places most likely to stay standing. 'I told you I heard something.' And she grinned like an idiot. She'd effectively cut our chances of getting out the UK by several hundred thousand per cent, and she was *pleased* about it. Then she teared up on me, like Santa Claus finding a baby to give a rattle to.

'Great,' I said. 'Hey, that's really great, Maude. You must be SO pleased with yourself.'

It was all I could do not to kick her in the teeth.

*

Let me tell you about Rowan.

He was three years old, right? The civil war was in full swing, snipers on the streets, nothing in the shops, health service dead. A war baby. Now you tell me what sort of total idiot moron woman actually goes and has a baby in the middle of *this*? I mean, how selfish can you get? I cannot even begin to tell you how angry it made me when I found out Mum was pregnant.

'So you're getting rid of it, right?' I said.

'Oh, no,' she said. 'No, no. How could I terminate a new life in the middle of all this death?'

We had a HUGE row about it. It went on for days. I didn't even know it was possible to have a row that big.

Dad was away, as usual. He only appeared long enough to get Mum up the duff and then he was away again. He's like, Oh, no, I don't have *time* to help my own family, I'm far too important for that. So here's a newborn baby and a half dead bully to look after. Really? I mean – *really*? We could hardly feed ourselves as it was. Mum was already in a mess. She was depressive, my mum. Definitely. Of course she wouldn't have it. She's like, Oh, no, nothing like that. I'm just depressed because of *circumstances*. Anyone would be depressed with all this going on, wouldn't they?

No, Mum. I'm not depressed and Maude's not and Dad's not. And you are!

But it was no use, say what you like, it was never anything to do with her. Neither she or Maude would have been even alive if it wasn't for me. But do I get a say? No way. I just get to play Mother while my actual mother is too busy being pregnant.

Of course Mum being Mum, she then went on to have the

worst pregnancy ever. The vomiting! She was a fountain of puke. Food was already getting short, and there she was vomming it all back up as soon as it went down. There was this time when Maude found a box full of canned peaches – a whole boxful! *Peaches!* They were dented but they were all good. Mum spooned them down herself every night for a week and then half an hour later – blurg! Up they'd all come.

'There go those peaches again,' said Maude. I could hardly speak, I was so angry. Every time I heard the tin opener going I wanted to run in and stab her with it. And did she learn? Did she leave the peaches for us? Of course she didn't. She kept trying and trying until they were all gone.

'But I love peaches,' she groaned. Yeah. So did I. Thanks, Mum.

When the vomiting stopped, the bloating began. When the bloating stopped, the high blood pressure started. If you ask me, for a woman to have a boy inside her – I mean an actual real boy, actually living inside her like some kind of alien parasite – it can't be right. It's poisonous, I reckon.

'Well, she managed it before OK, didn't she?' said Maude. I didn't even bother answering. I have to deal with that sort of thing all the time.

Mum could have had a termination easily. There were still clinics open. It wasn't like she was religious or anything. I told her. 'Look around you,' I said. 'Bombs going off all over the place. Militias roaming the street. Racists and supremacists running around. And – you're married to a Black man! You have Black kids!' Well, it's all right for her, she's white. But me? You can lie about your religion or your politics, but you can never lie about the colour of your skin.

Let me think. We live in an absolute racist hellhole. How can we make it even worse? Oh – I know! Let's bring another *Black* person into the world in case the racists need a little extra target practice, why don't you?

Great. And to add insult to injury, when he was born, the little wretch was actually *white*, pretty nearly. I mean, how's that? Really! An almost-white Black brother. The little toad. I could have strangled him at birth.

I know what you're thinking. You're thinking, There she goes. Moaning about her brother. The usual. Brothers and sisters, eh? Always moaning about each other but underneath they adore one another really.

No. Really *no*. I genuinely did hate him. I know it wasn't his fault. He didn't ask to be brought into the world, did he? If he'd been able to see what he was coming into, he'd have said no, I expect. I certainly would've. Well, I'm sorry about it. I really am. But still, all that notwithstanding . . . yes. I did actually, genuinely hate him.

But surely, you say, *surely* I was pleased to see my little baby brother had survived? Surely I was going to look after him.

Excuse me? Can you imagine how *hard* it was going to be to get away from here anyway? Militias, roadblocks. Radical beardie Muslims. White supremacist Christian maniacs. Bombs. Refugees. And now I had a toddler with me. On what planet is that good news? And it's not just any normal three-year-old we're talking about here – it's a precious, whining, spoilt, bad-tempered little toad of a three-year-old. To look at him, you might think butter wouldn't melt. Cute? Yes, cute as kittens – if you didn't know him like I did. Believe me, this is a kid unable to think of *anything* except himself.

So me and Maude had an ENORMOUS row about what to do with Rowan. I wanted to do the sensible thing, which was to hand him over to a charity, who'd find him a nice family to live with. Cutesy three-year-old, whiteish toddler, wants rescuing from hunger and despair by loving family. Come on! This is a war zone! It's our duty to make sure he has the best chances possible.

'He's your brother,' she said.

'Yeah, that's why I'm doing my best to find a decent home for him,' I said. There were a dozen organisations who'd be falling over themselves to take him on . . . and help us out on our hazardous journey by compensating us for our noble sacrifice. Come on. I mean – COME ON!

'We promised your mum,' said Maude, and she looked away as if that was the end of the conversation. As if promises were real. As if they were made out of steel and concrete. Like if you dropped one on your foot, you'd break your toe.

I was furious.

'You go with him, you go on your own,' I said.

'He's *your* brother,' she said again, cool as you like. It was one of the things I hated about Maude – she was always so cool.

'A brother?' I said. 'What does that even *mean*? Why should I be responsible for him just because we have the same parents? I told Mum not to have him, but she did anyway. He's not my fault and if something's not your fault, it's not your responsibility.'

'He's a person, not an argument.'

'I don't care.'

'Yes, you do.'

'I do *not*, Maude. I really do not. You know how much I hate him.'

'No, you don't.'

'Yes I do. I really, really, *really* do,' I said through clenched teeth.

She scowled, and farted. We might be guests, but we were still on the chickpea diet. 'Whatever. I promised Mum that if anything happened to her, I'd look after you and Rowan. End of.'

See? I even had to share my own mother with her. What a cow!

We argued and argued, I talked sense, she talked cojones. I talked practicalities, she talked pie in the sky. But it was no use. Rubblehead just had to have her own way. And the annoying thing was, I *still* had more chance of getting out with her than I did on my own, even with the whiny one coming along. This was going to be an extremely dangerous trip. Maude had trained with the FNA. She'd been on courses. She can shoot a gun, she knows first aid, she can drive. She's pretty. She's *white*. She has contacts and perfect tits.

Sickening though it was, I had no choice but to give up on it.

5

The plan was to get to Hull. Maude had promised my mum she'd look after me, so she was coming that far, then she was going to come back and face certain death in the Fight for Freedom, while I jumped on a ferry to free Amsterdam, city of my dreams, to get laid, drunk and stoned, not necessarily in that order.

But first, we had to get out of Manchester.

The route out of town was dictated by local politics. Manchester was never really like just one place, but it was seriously in bits and pieces these days. Some parts were still torn about with fighting; it wasn't safe to walk down the street. Other parts weren't too bad. Our bit had had some very heavy fighting in the past, but since the FNA got control, it was OK. They'd chased the opposition away, got rid of the snipers, started getting better supplies into the shops. Phone and wi-fi was still hopeless, though, because they didn't control the air and as soon as they put a mast up or got the power back on, it got bombed flat.

But still – you could move about. If it wasn't for the empty shops, the rubble, the craters in the roads and the bullet holes in the buildings from a couple of years ago when the racists had tried to come in, you could almost think things were normal. Ha, ha, ha.

Going east through the city was the most direct, but also the most dangerous. That part of town was splintered into God-knows-how-many militias. Christian militia, Muslim militia, fascist militia, commie militia, each one controlling their own little patch of streets and estates. Snipers everywhere. Kidnapping. Forget it.

North Manc was even worse, if anything, because that was pretty much run by a bunch of right-wing racists – not the Bloods. Not yet. We Northerners have our own scumbags to deal with, and the bunch who'd managed to take control of north Manchester were the BNLF – the British National Liberation Front. Good old fashioned UK racists. My favourite kind. They didn't care about God, but what they did have in common with the Bloods was they hated brownskins.

North was out, east was out. West was the wrong direction. We had to go south, which was run by the FNA, which was supported by the Rusholme Muslim Council. Down to Stockport, then we'd circle round underneath Manchester, across the Peaks towards Barnsley and Doncaster, that way. Long way, but best way. Now that Birmingham had fallen, the Bloods were advancing fast up the west side of the country, but they were much slower on the east.

A lot of those towns on our route were in the hands of the FNA, more or less. As was Maude. Contacts, see? She had her uses. We had to move fast, that's all, because in a situation like this, things were changing from day to day. You could never tell. All you knew was, something was going to go wrong. You didn't know what it was, and how exactly it was going to make a mess of your life. You just knew it was going to happen.

Mum didn't die a moment too soon. With a bit of luck, this time next week I could be sitting in a cafe in Amsterdam, stoned out of my head, being chatted up by a tall, lean Dutchman. They're descended from mammoth hunters, the tall ones. Did you know that?

Imagine . . .

I spent my time waiting for Rowan to get better, gathering supplies and repacking my backpack. I decided to add a few outfits to get me through – and before you think I was being ridiculously girlie, let me dissuade you of your prejudicial stereotyping. I won't argue that I had a few skirts and dresses and various items of summer wear in there, but it was far more than that.

Maude was on at me to go disguised as a boy to avoid attracting attention.

'Incognito, Marti,' she said, looking me up and down.

'I'm not wearing anything showy,' I pointed out.

'You don't need to,' she said. That was just plain rude. Rude – but true. I'd already decided on my refugee outfit. It was plain, but very stylish. Combats. Tailored waist, button-down epaulets, trousers narrowing down to the ankle, all topped off with a matching cap. Maude hadn't seen that yet.

Maude always said how lucky I am that I can look like a boy, because most girls can't. Thanks. Always looks on the bright side, our Maudie. If she tried it, she'd only look even sexier than she already does. You can't hide a shape like that. If Maude ever got caught by the Bloods or some of the other little groups, she'd get raped. It's what they do.

Me, I've always looked like a boy, even though I most emphatically am not. Lucky, huh?

We had other stuff to get before we left, now that Rowan was part of the plan. Maude got hold of one of those three-wheeled pushchairs. Kind of off-road pushchairs. I always thought they looked stupid back in the pre-bomb days, the days of proper pavements and smooth surfaces, but it was going to be useful now because in Manchester at that time, even the roads were off-road. Bombs apart, no one had been on pothole duty for an age. I found us a couple of baby carriers, which were probably going to be even more useful. But it was food that was the main thing.

Rowan has these allergies. Yeah – I know. Allergies in a war zone. Doesn't it make you want to eat your own teeth? We had to get oats and special biscuits and stuff, because of nuts. We even managed to get our hands on some gluten-free bread for the little fusspot. Gluten-free bread! We bought that – we actually *spent money* on gluten-free bread. Even now, when I think that we had to spend all that money on gluten-free bread for the precious, it makes me seethe. There's more, but I can't talk about it. It winds me up too much to even think about it.

Maude had her own stuff for 'the mission'. The FNA had this kit they gave to people if they were trying to get out – bibles and prayer books if we wandered into regime territory, so we could pretend to be soaked in the Blood of Christ.

'We may bump into Bloods. We'll need to show them we're on their side,' she said.

'Showing them bibles isn't going to convince them,' I said. Because the Bloods, they're like, Catholics? Stone 'em to death. Prods? Heretics, cut out their tongues. Really, they get up to that sort of thing. I'd seen it on my phone. It's not enough to be a Christian, you have to be the right sort of Christian, or you're more or less as bad as Hitler. There are no degrees of badness for people like that. You're either Blood or else you're the spawn of Satan.

Maudie had a whole load of FNA bumf. Pamphlets outlining how to talk your way past the Bloods. There was a lot to learn. For instance, if one of them asked you, 'Are you one with the Blood of Jesus?', you didn't say, 'Yes.' You said, 'The Blood of Jesus is in all of us, brother.' Stuff like that. If you got it wrong – heretic! Gang rape her now! Yes, they do that. They get round it by making you marry each one in turn, then divorcing you for adultery in time for the next one. You know, I'm not a Christian myself, but you get the feeling that these guys were kind of missing the spirit of the thing.

And weapons. Yeah, she had a gun. One of those pistols where you shove a cartridge up the handle and get ten or twelve shots. Very cool. She got it from the FNA and she'd actually used it in action defending our patch against some nasties from the east. I was surprised they were letting her keep it now that she was leaving. But the thing you really need to know about Maude, she has this secret weapon that gains her favours certain other members of our sex don't have – her vagina.

I offered to look after it for her – the gun, not the vagina, although I'd have had that too, if I could.

'Back off, Marti,' she said.

That was Rubblehead. There was no telling her anything.

We set off without ceremony *a whole week* after Rowan had been dug out of the rubble. The magnolia tree in front of our house was in flower. I'd known that tree all my life, it was gorgeous every spring. A couple of branches had been broken off where the roof slid down, but it was still pretty. Thomas was giving a singing lesson to one of the fat beardy baritones he fancies so much, practising scales in a big brown voice. I couldn't make out a word, never could, even when it was in English. Thomas leaned out the window and waved goodbye, and the beardy baritone stuck his head out too.

'Goodbye, Goodbye, See you in the f*****g springtime,' he sang. I made that out all right.

That was our send off. Pretty weird in the middle of a war zone. I thought it was great! A few years before, there'd have been a crowd to see me off, but all my friends were either dead, kidnapped and imprisoned, or abroad.

And was I sorry to say goodbye to the place where I grew up? Was I sad? Did I murmur, 'See you again old friends' to the magnolia tree and the remains of the familiar houses as I passed them by for the last time?

No, I did not. Manchester had stopped being the place

I belonged, years before. If I never saw it one more time in a thousand years, it would be too soon.

Our route was up the Mauldeth Road, through Burnage, out on the Didsbury Road at Heaton Mersey, around Stockport and off across to the Peaks. That last part of the route was still unsure – there was fighting along the Snake's Pass from time to time, but the main problem was from the air. If you wanted to get to Europe from the north-west, you had to go over the Snake's Pass, or the A628, and so it was an obvious target for anyone who wanted to polish off a few refugees. There were no other major roads across those hills, but if you went further south there were some little roads, more trees, less traffic. But it was slower. We were still arguing about which way to go as we trollied along the Mauldeth Road. Maude wanted to cut the risk and go south-east; I'd had enough of going in circles, I wanted the more direct route after Stockport – straight across towards Hull and on, on, to the city of sin.

Things were pretty bad-tempered right from the start, when Maude saw my nicely ironed combats. They were classy numbers – I got them from Harvey Nicks when the Arndale got bombed a few months before. They had a powder blue background with deep green camouflage splotches, of which every fourth or fifth one was pink.

'Pink camouflages?' she hissed at me.

'They're not pink,' I said. 'Just bits of them are.'

'F**k's sake, Marti! Those are the most girlie combats you could buy. Just stop it, will you?'

So she was sulking right at the start, but I wasn't having any. I have my principles. I had a change of combats in case I needed something a bit more military later on. We hadn't even left our street at that point. And then things got a whole lot worse . . .

Yeah, what rotten luck I had that day. We were about fifteen minutes out, just round about Ladybarn, when my phone went off. My secret phone. I mean, how unlucky can you get? I must surely be the unluckiest person in the world. My Sylvester ringtone, that I never put on my other phone, rang out for all to hear. There was no chance of Maude mistaking it for anything else.

Well, she looked at me and I looked at her. It was so embarrassing. I thought I might *die* of embarrassment. I was just checking to see what was going on – there was no sim in it, turned out it was some kind of timer that I must have set by accident – when she launched herself at me. Next thing you knew we were both rolling around on the ground, scrapping for the phone.

'It's mine, it's mine, it's mine!' I was shouting, and, 'No it f*****g isn't, you lying cow!' she was yelling. Maude is a trained fighter, but I have the upper-body strength, so I could have easily won if she hadn't kicked me in the face and bust my nose. I dropped the phone and clutched my face, and she snatched it up from the ground. Although I'm taller and stronger, Maude was always the one with the cool head, plus the training. Plus of course she had right on her side, which helps. So I lost the fight and instead I threw a gigantic tantrum, right there in front of the bombed out Co-op. I flounced, I stropped, I raged, I wept. I told you I never swear. I did then. I swore and swore and swore and swore. I lost it utterly. I howled and raged. I went for her, we had a fight. She won again.

It's not fair, is it? I'm at the bottom of every single heap. Find a heap – I'm there at the bottom of it. Why? Why me?

'You don't care if I die,' I wept.

'You have one life, Marti,' she said. 'This,' she went on, waggling the phone temptingly in the air, '*This* could save thousands, maybe tens of thousands, maybe *hundreds* of thousands of lives.' She stuck it in her bra and patted it. 'You're a cow. We go south to Huntingdon.'

'Listen to me,' I said, trying not to cry. 'You do this, Maude. You go all the way down south, right into the hands of the Bloods if that's what you want to do. But you go on your own and you take Rowan with you. I mean it. It's all right for you. Spoiled little white girl. Look at me. Look! I'm everything the Bloods hate. All they need is one glimpse of me and I'm dead.'

She looked at me like I was a piece of doggy-do under her foot and gave me her parting shot. 'Tell you what, Marti. You break your promise to your mum, you break your promise to your dad, you desert your little brother – what's your life worth? Nothing. But come with me and look after your brother and try to help fix your dad's life's work, what are you worth then? *Everything.* You need to ask yourself how you're going to live with yourself if you dump us. I'm going down south. You better come, you hear me? You be there for us, like I'm always there for you when you need me, or I swear I'll never speak to you again.'

'And what exactly would I want to say to a dead racist bitch?'
I yelled after her.

As if I cared. Stupid, stupid, stupid! Even now, just the
thought of it makes me want to spit.

6

I was furious. Of all the places in the world I didn't want to go to, the ERAC at Huntingdon was right up there at the top of the list. People like me, we have to fight so hard to be who we are. All my life, people wanted me to be someone else. My friends at school, my family. Even strangers on the street who don't know anything about me think they know better. My dad, even after he accepted me, was always pining for the little boy he lost. And then just when you've finally made it clear to those around you that actually, this isn't just a passing fad – like, this is who I am, finally! – what happens? Here's my best friend, no less, the only person close to me in the whole world, actually telling me I have to go down to the worst place in existence – the place that will strip me of everything I am, or could be or ever was. Because I tell you, if I ever ended up inside the ERAC, that was going to be the end of me. My ideas, my politics, my history, my gender, my sexuality – gone, all gone. There would simply be nothing left.

No one's sure who commissioned the ERAC. It's run by Google. Remember them? They used to be really big on the internet. It's right by one of the big US air bases so it was probably the US who started it. If you asked most people what goes on there, they'd say, Oh, torture, beatings, terror. The usual. Maybe that's true. In fact, it almost certainly is true. But the ERAC is much more than that.

It's an experiment. You know that saying about how history is always written by the winners, yeah? Well, in Huntingdon, they don't just rewrite the history books. They rewrite *people*.

They worked out how to identify thoughts first. Then they worked out how to delete them, then how to implant them. Most of the initial work was done at Manchester Uni, according to my dad, who was a student there doing his PhD in A.I. when it was all starting up. They were all really excited about it in his department, thought they were finding new ways of treating mental illness. You see how it could have been? A brand new mind for the crazies among us. Or even the insecure. Or the unhappy or the shy or the anxious, which, let's face it, is most of us.

When Google came along to buy it up, the guys at Manchester were made up about that, because although it was no longer theirs, there was suddenly all this money to play with. But of course they were being utterly naïve. What they'd been hoping for wasn't even a tiny bit what Google wanted. Google didn't care about a cure for the sick. What they wanted was profits. And where do you get the best profits? The military, of course. My mum was right when she said that cost goes out the window when it comes to warfare.

Next thing you know, my dad and his fellow let's-help-mankind mates were out, forbidden to say, do or barely even think about the work they'd done, and the US military was busy using their tech to develop mind-changers, mind-readers, mind-your-own-businessers, you name it. They weren't interested in people who had crazy thoughts at all – they were interested in people who had *bad* thoughts. You know? Bad thoughts like, What a bag of sickos the Americans are. Or the commies wanting to nationalise your daddy's private business empire. Or, What a good idea the NHS was. *Those* kind of bad thoughts.

And hallelujah, brothers and sisters! Think of what you could do with that! Peace on Earth, brotherhood among all mankind. No wonder the Christians went for it so bad. Who needs war when you control what people think? Conflict, disagreement, Islam, Buddhists, terrorism – all gone! Pinko lefties get turned into decent rednecks overnight! Now let's just have a little chat about that oil price, shall we . . . ?

While all that was going on, the US economy was bombing – had been for years, let's face it. The debt was getting bigger, the economy was getting smaller. Then one day, the dollar collapsed. The US military woke up and found themselves no longer being paid, so some of them decided it was the destiny of the US to rule things in a much better way, a much *whiter* way than heretofore. After they won the civil war at home, they busied themselves sorting out the rest of the world, and among the various other jolly things they did, one was to install a pro-US government over here: the Bloods. And Lo! The ERAC at Huntingdon came to pass, so they could make good Christians out of human rubbish like you and me. Queers go in one end and they come out straight. Islamists turn into good Christians, black people go in and come out – well, not white, of course. But racism doesn't exist any more. *It never did.* We just *realise* that we're inferior, just like our nice white cousins have been telling us all along.

And the Muslims who've lived here for sixty years want to go home and the gays think they're sick and trans people just want to stop being so confused.

All that costly military hardware – unnecessary! You don't have to fight anyone. You don't even have to argue with them. You just rewrite them and your enemies become your friends. It's great. Hallelujah! All the Bloods need now is the second coming and everything'll be just like they want it.

That's the aim anyway. At the moment it's still in the experimental stage. And that's what the ERAC at Huntingdon is all about.

My dad was appalled, partly because he had been involved in developing it, but also because his sister, Grace, my aunt, died in a mental hospital. Crazy runs in our family – you might have noticed. The poor old codger really thought he was going to do good, and instead his baby turns out to be a dreadful monster. So him and some of the team from Manchester Uni started work on ways of undoing the damage done by their own invention. Basically, the way the drones flying over the ERAC work, they don't wipe the old memories out – they just block them. My dad and his mates wanted to develop software that could unblock those old memories and block the new stuff instead. 'Reinstalling the truth,' they called it.

That's what the phone was about. The software they developed was installed on it.

My dad's mates disappeared one by one over the years. He was the last one on the team. If by any remote chance he was still alive, my dad, who was just about the most militant Black man you ever met, he'd be some kind of Uncle Tom by now, working for the Bloods. He'd have told them all about the software so's they could nullify it, which meant there really was *no* point even trying any more. A point which I made to Maude, and which she steadfastly ignored, on the grounds that even a small chance was better than no chance at all.

So that's the ERAC. Can you even begin to imagine what they'd do to me if they ever got their hands on me? And yet that's where Maude, lovely Maude, who's practically my own sister, wanted me to go. All of which is why, once we get to Stockport, Maude's going one way and I'm going another. Because while she's the heroic type, who cares not for her own safety and only lives for the safety and happiness of those not yet born, I am of another persuasion. I am of the persuasion that cares for those who live on this Earth right now, and of those who live on this Earth right now, there is one among them that I care the very most for.

Me.

See? I told you you weren't going to like me.

7

If you were to ask me how I felt about abandoning my baby brother and my best friend – my only friend – then I would say, actually, I felt furious that I'd been forced into taking that sort of action.

'That *you*, a cis white person, expect someone like *me* to go down south into the arms of a bunch of lynching, raping, murdering, transphobic, racist bastards is just astonishing.' That's how I put it to Maude. And she rolled her eyes. Yes, she rolled her eyes. Like I was kicking up a fuss about nothing. Well, that's white privilege for you. They just don't get it. But it showed me one thing, I can tell you. I was on my own – then, now and for ever. And if I was going to be on my own, I was going to be on my own somewhere *nice*. That's it. Forget the rest. Forget my dad. Look what happened to him. Forget my mum – look what happened to her. That's it. I'm the last of my line, it's my duty to carry on.

What's that you say? Rowan? What about Rowan?

Well, *what* about Rowan? Maude thinks she's family. She can look after him. Speaking of Rowan, that fight me and Maude had on the pavements of the Mauldeth Road set him off into his favourite activity: wailing and screaming. It took Maude twenty minutes or more to calm him down. Off we set again, both of us seething away like chip pans; Rowan's eyes wide open, staring from one to the other of us, sucking away on his dum-dum like some kind of disgusting arthropod trying to feed on a piece of waste plastic. Which, as far as I was concerned, he was. Maude had my phone, wouldn't give it back for fear I'd trample on it. We got all the way to Heaton Mersey without exchanging a single word, except for me muttering, 'Bitch,' under my breath. Every time I did it, Maude closed her eyes and did some private seething of her own for a couple of minutes. Never said a word and just carried on walking, shoving the pushchair up the road and trying not to bump the poor injured cockroach in it too much.

Burnage was no problem – there'd been a fight with some racists there recently, and the FNA won, which was how it usually came about in that part of town. Rowan perked up – he was actually being quite good, which was unusual for him. The thing is, he never used to get out much, so travelling along an open road, there was so much for him to see. Except that he kept asking after Mum, and having a cry because she wasn't there, which was horrible. I was trying not to think about that.

So we were doing OK. And then . . .

Roadblock. It was an FNA roadblock, so we weren't too worried at first. Maude had her FNA documents, which she was waving in everyone's face, but it was no good – they wouldn't let us through. You see what it's like? Twenty minutes and a couple of miles later and everything had already changed.

In the end we decided to double back round and go via Parrs Wood, maybe even go right back to Fallowfield and up the motorway if we had to.

We made it as far as Parrs Wood and . . . roadblock! And this time you could see what was going on. Colour was going on. Mainly Asian Muslims but plenty of Black folk, too. Thousands of them. They'd made it through Stockport, got part of the way down the road towards Manc – and that was it. There they were, sitting on the road looking miserable, or exhausted, or angry or just plain scared, or all four. Penned in. And we were penned in with them.

Yes, the Muslim hordes. They'd marched all the way from Birmingham, Wolverhampton, maybe even London, some of them. We pushed our way through the crowds to get to the FNA who were in charge of the roadblock, where there were some furious arguments going on between the Muslim FNA, who wanted to let their people through, and the white FNA, who didn't. Nobody seemed to really know what was going on, which was entirely as per normal. There were no orders coming down from the leadership, wherever they were, but you can bet that exactly the same arguments with the same people on each side were happening there, too.

Maude tried waving her papers in the faces of the FNA militia – dragging me forcibly by my elbow, I should tell you, because that was a place I had no wish to be. There were weapons pointing in all directions. The white FNA were arguing with the Asians, both the ones on the other side of the roadblock and the ones who were their comrades this side. Things were very, very heated. But Maude, hand it to her, she was shouting away, demanding attention. When that didn't work, she hit one of the senior officers on the side of the head with her papers.

That worked. Everyone stopped shouting and they all looked down at us. I have to say, we must have looked pretty weird. The pretty one was dressed in a FNA uniform with a tight belt around her tiny waist. The ugly one was in a set of partly pink hi-fash combats, with a tight stretchy top which showed off her two favourite assets. I was also pushing a pushchair with a baby in it.

'What?' said the soldier.

'Mission to the ERAC, Huntingdon. We're carrying important assets. You have to let us through,' insisted Maude.

The guy glanced at the papers. Then one of his Asian comrades started yelling again and poking him in the chest, and . . . he let us through. Yes, he did. I think he only did it to annoy the Asian guy. We walked through, and off we went again, leaving them behind more angry than ever.

On we went, rejoicing. We got a quarter of a mile or so before, Lo! We came across the real reason why we'd been let through.

Another roadblock! That other one had just been to hold back the firstcomers. This was the real one. I thought it had been a horde behind that first one. I was wrong. It turns out I didn't really know what a horde was. Behind this roadblock, that was the real horde.

There were people as far as you could see. Every available space was heaving with them – all over the motorway roundabout, up the M60, down the road to Stockport. Thousands, tens of thousands, maybe hundreds of thousands. It was a flood. Every single one of them was on the run from the

Bloods, every single one of them was desperate to get through and none of them were going anywhere. At the back of them, more were arriving every hour, more and more and more, creating a bigger and bigger bottleneck. They all wanted food, drink, the loo. They wanted *everything*, and there wasn't anything like enough of any of it.

The FNA had orders not to let anyone in or out, but there weren't enough of them to hold the horde back for ever. It was a disaster in the making. And meanwhile, somewhere behind them, and no one knew how far, the Bloods were on their way. For the refugees, that was going to mean either a massacre or a concentration camp, which as far as I can tell, is just a slow version of a massacre, anyway. So things were very, very edgy.

Among the Asian hordes were the other smaller hordes. Black people, queer people, Jewish people. The Bloods didn't hate the Jews, they just booted them out of the country and told them to go to Israel, but a lot of the Jews weren't too keen on that either since they'd lived here since time began anyway. And there were a whole host of radicals, revolutionaries, Catholics, Baptists, Buddhists. All on the run, all desperate to get away, desperate to keep moving – and all of them stuck.

There was only one person there who the Bloods hated, who was going the other way, as far as I could tell. That person was the very last one of them all who should have been doing that, because they encapsulated in themselves everything that the Bloods hated – race, sexuality, belief, gender, the lot.

Me.

There were actually a number of very normal-looking white folk trying to sneak to the south as well. Not because they actually agreed with the Bloods, practically no one sane did that, but on the grounds that the war was pretty much over down there (for now!) and you were perfectly safe so long as you were the right colour and were prepared to say whatever the Bloods wanted you to.

But of course they were out of luck as well. The FNA had been told not to let *anyone* through in either direction. Including traitors. So that's what they were doing.

And all the time the bottleneck was getting bigger, and bigger and bigger. And everyone was getting more and more frustrated and more and more angry. And the Bloods were getting closer and closer and closer. And out of all those hundreds of thousands of people, not one of them was having any fun.

We found ourselves a spot, put up our tarp, which Maude the Clever had packed, sat under it, tried not to eat and drink too much, and waited for something to happen. One thing I've learned about war, it's the most boring thing in the world, right up to the moment when it suddenly becomes far too exciting. Know what I mean?

But not Maude. She wiped down her army fatigues, tightened the belt around her tiny wee waist, opened a few buttons down the front and announced she was off to negotiate our passage. My guess was, that wasn't the only passage that was going to those negotiations. Maude is such a slut! But you have to hand it to her. That's all it took, a few opened buttons, a tight belt and bingo! Every head turned, men and women, but let's face it, especially the men. The beardie Muslims, the young, the old. Anyone with a hormone left in them.

I don't blame her. If I had a bod like hers, I'd be a slut, too.

While Maude was out slutting, I was left at home looking after the poop machine. Rowan. Yes – really! He was three and he was *still* pooing himself. He wouldn't let me put a nappy on him, just ran around, pooped himself, then came running back to be cleaned up. By me. On that first day he did it three times. Three times, in one day? See, we fed him too much. Something to do with the allergies I expect. The third time, I didn't feel like retching my way through another set of kecks, so I told him just to ignore it.

'They say I smell,' he said, looking over his shoulder towards his playmates.

'Ignore them. They're bullies,' I said. I should know, I've spent most of my life being bullied. But when Maude got back in the evening, the poo had turned his bum red raw and I got no end of grief. It's like *Alien*, only not with acid blood – with acid poo.

So that was me for the next few days – scraping poo off Rowan's poo extruder and making sure he didn't get kidnapped by some weird, poo-loving paedophile, who probably doesn't exist in the first place. What fun! Although, to be fair, I did have some proper, actual fun with him. Little Rowan, like I say, had been kept at home by Mum so much of the time that he was actually still at the point where everything was an adventure. He was in a state of such innocence and actual downright ignorance about the world, even I found it kinda cute.

'Look, Rowan. Spider!'

'Spida.' And he stared at it like I'd just shown him a wonderful treasure. Which, let's face it, I had.

53

'Butterfly.'

'Burrfly.'

'Bicycle! Baby! Man with a funny hat! Beetle! Fountain!' I did that one by shaking a bottle of fizzy water I'd bought. Poor little thing. Mum was so terrified that he'd get stolen or killed, he never went out and she was too depressed to entertain him much at home.

Maude was a lot happier with me that evening.

'Maybe he's not spoilt. Maybe he's just bored,' she said. Which might have been true but then I could also say that my circumstances have made me the cow I am, but it doesn't make me any nicer, does it? Even so, I was a bit more on his side for a while and I was even reconsidering leaving him with Maude and taking him with me to Amsterdam as soon as the roadblock was down, but then he blew it utterly by waking me up early one morning and peeing all over my sleeping bag. With me in it.

'Fou'tin, fou'tin! Look, Marti, fou'tin!' he screamed. Oh, he knew what he was doing, the little pee-er. He was laughing his head off – until I smacked his bum and shoved him out of the tent. Don't talk to me about smacking, no one ever smacked me and *not* being smacked didn't do me any good, did it? Then he went wailing around the place like the world had ended. There wasn't water to wash the sleeping bags, so I had to hang them out and sit in the pee smell under the tarp, and sleep in it at nights, while he went off to play with the crowd of kids who were hanging around the camp. Suits me. The little pee-er.

*

We did have our fifteen minutes of excitement that day when mobile coverage suddenly kicked in. Most people had their mobiles turned off to save battery – you never knew when you were going to get to charge it. So it started off with just one or two phones going off, and then everyone cottoned on and whipped their phones out, and off it went all together ... ringtones and text alerts that had been hanging around for days flying around all over the place, everything bleeping, dinging, bits of tunes, buzz buzz buzz. It was hilarious. And everyone's ringing up their family and their mates and trying to shout over one another, noses stuck in their phones trying to work out who's alive, who's dead, who made it out, who's still in there. Me too. I'd got myself a new phone in Manc while we were waiting for Rowan to get better. So when I saw everyone whipping out their phones and studying them dead hard and typing and making calls, I checked out mine to see what was going on.

I had a few messages. The one from my friend Conor, who'd made it to Ireland. He has an auntie in County Clare. He was going, *Come on over, Marti, it's great, there's cars everywhere and fresh milk and butter everyday!* I was like, *Dairy products?* Are you kidding me? And I actually had messages from my brother in Amsterdam, which made my little heart leap for a second – before it came crashing down like a fallen angel at my feet.

Where you at, bruv? Hey, bruv – you still alive?

Bruv. Boy, was he in for a shock.

And then, *Hey, Mart – I might be coming over soon, keep an eye out for me!*

I was like ... Noooooooooo. I was on my phone going, *No no no!*

I *needed* him in Amsterdam! But no answer. The trouble is, my brothers Adam and Aiyden both converted to Islam a few years ago. Dad was furious – started calling them the Ishmaels. Ishmael 1 and Ishmael 2. The whole family fell out about it. They grew beards and started calling themselves Muhammad and Ali. Dad refused to call them that, so they wouldn't talk to him until he did. His mother, my gran, who had wisely fled to Ireland some years ago, stopped talking to *him* until he talked to them. It was a mess.

Ishmael 1, AKA Muhammad, AKA Adam came over here to fight for the Birmingham Islamic Foundation a year ago. We hadn't heard a word from him for months, which you'd think would put Ishmael 2, AKA Ali, AKA Aiyden off, but no way.

Me, I learn to welcome martyrdom into my life, he texted me. Martyrdom. Everyone else calls it being dead. They call it martyrdom. And . . . I learn? *I learn?* He never used to talk like that before. *I save a virgin for you in Paradise, bruv*, he said. Well, thanks. When I pop my cherry, I want it to be with someone who knows their way around, not some stupid virgin who's as ignorant as I am. Know what I mean? Poor Aiyden! He hasn't seen me for so long, he has no idea about me. He's in for a shock when he meets me, I can tell you.

This is my life. What kind of morons live in Amsterdam, the drug and sex capital of the western world and become *Islamic fundamentalists?*

My brothers. Just my luck!

There were a few texts from other mates. Jay, Skinner, Charlene, Alexa – all of them out of it now. There was a text from Lara in Birmingham, where the Bloods had arrived a few weeks earlier.

According to her, the fighting was still going on, but it was just mopping up little pockets of resistance. There were troops moving further north, which meant the push to Manchester could happen any day now – as if we didn't already know.

Nothing from my dad. That was six months now. I still hoped. I never stopped checking whenever I got coverage, even though I knew it was useless.

Two more days went by, then a third. I was going crazy. Maude was still 'negotiating' but none of it had paid off yet. Rowan was off with his little mates every day, which was just as well as I'd run out of things he'd never seen or heard before. The parents of the other kids kept their eye on him along with their own, so I could lie under the tarp and read. And queue. There was a lot of queueing going on. The Red Cross and other charities turned up, doling out food and medicines and so on. We weren't doing too badly, because Maude was using her contacts and her assets to get us supplies from the FNA as well, so a lot of folk had it worse off than us.

Rowan was having the time of his life. He never even knew more than about three people in the world before that. Me, I slept, queued and read. I reread Malcolm X, and the ten commandments of the new Black Power movement. One day, brothers and sisters, one day. I reread Juno and listened to my tunes. I went on a book hunt around the camp and got a few more, including *Alice in Wonderland*, which I'd never read before. It is the *campest* book I ever read – Lewis Carroll was *definitely* queer. Trust me. It made me feel all kinda militant, so

I took off the military-style combats that I'd changed into for the mud and so on, and dressed girlie, in my very short skirt – the pussy pelmet – and a low-cut top. I got a lot of surprised looks from people, especially the beardie Muslims, and quite a few angry ones as well.

'I have children here,' one of them hissed at me.

'That beard doesn't suit you either, and if *you* can look ridiculous, so can I,' I told him. Which I was rather pleased with.

On the third day we had some more excitement – tanks! Two tanks, Boris 62s, so British, but they had the stars and stripes stencilled on the sides. You could tell they weren't Blood tanks at a distance because they were making their way up the M60 towards us and no one was running for their lives. The motorway was so packed with people, they were making slow progress. After a bit you could hear a loudspeaker telling everyone to clear the way – 'Move to one side, move to one side everyone. It's OK, we're here to sort this out . . . move to one side . . .' – in an American accent. And cheering, as people realised that they were on their side.

Everyone crowded round them, which made it even harder for them to move. They were the first tanks I'd seen since they all went running south a few years ago when London was under attack.

I know what you're thinking. US troops in British tanks? What's that all about?

When the US defaulted on the dollar, they ended up having their own civil war over there, which, as you know, was won by the South this time – way, way to the right of anything they'd ever had before. And Lo! It came to pass that over here in the UK the

Brotherhood of the Blood of Jesus, which was a tiddly little group of badly armed nutjobs, became funded up to the hilt overnight and started obliterating and smiting their enemies with helicopter gunships, artillery, and tanks, etc. And the rest of us were verily squashed, smited, written out, and generally done over big time.

And it also came to pass that quite a few of the US troops in the UK, the ones in the US bases over here, weren't at all happy with what was going on either back home or over here. The Black ones, for example. A lot of liberal whites, too, who were kinda keen on democracy and freedom, started to fight over here against the Bloods. Others, like this crew, didn't take sides, they just liked soldiering. They were calling themselves US Forces for Freedom. But they were actually following the good old US custom of making money out of other people's misery. In other words, they were mercenaries.

It turned out that some of the better-off Asians from Birmingham had paid them to protect the refugees on the road. Of course, once they realised that, everyone was clustered around the tanks, cheering, wanting to shake their hands and beg, which made their progress even slower. From when we first heard them to the point where they actually arrived at the barricade, I'd say it took them about three hours to cover maybe a mile. But when they got there, they turned the turret round so that big, big gun was pointing straight at FNA HQ and ordered them to lift the barricade.

To cut a long story short, it didn't make any difference. The FNA didn't have anything that could take a tank out, but they did have thousands of the very people the UFF had been paid to protect. While the tanks were crawling at 0 mph up the motorway, the FNA spent their time chaining a few hundred of them to the HQ and various other targets. The tank could have just gone forward and crawled over the barricade but if they did that, they'd crush the hostages.

The tank commander got down to negotiate.

'Listen, my friend – we're just the forward force. We have another *four* of these babies coming up behind,' he said, patting his vehicle fondly. 'You might as well open up for us now. Save you a whole lotta trouble later on.'

'If they're here before Christmas, they get a cracker,' the FNA guy said, and his men cracked up laughing. There wasn't anything moving up and down that motorway. Stalemate! We all had to just sit back down and wait, either for the other tanks to turn up, or for the tank guys to decide to roll over anyway, or for the FNA to just let 'em through. Which, when all was said and done, they were going to have to do sooner or later.

Great. So we sat for *another* two days. What can I say? It rained. Food was running out. Everyone was pooing and peeing. Can you imagine it? And all the time, the crowd was growing even more monumental – maybe half a million or more, who knows, spreading all over the motorway, backing up into Stockport. It was turning into the mother of all refugee camps. The FNA were trying to herd people into holding points in the playing fields and farmland around the schools and by the river, but they were meeting a lot of resistance, because people wanted to be off as soon as they could.

And still they came. The whole place stank. We had a heavy rain shower a couple of times and . . . well. It was difficult to tell where the mud ended and the poo began, put it like that. We'd been on the road for five days and we'd done about two miles. Great! Flying start!

We were in the same boat as everyone else now, running out of food. I had to go off looking for it. Rice, I wanted rice. It's dry goods, easy to transport, it keeps, and isn't going to make Rowan's bottom explode. People were feeding the little idiot all sorts of unsuitable things. Nuts! Where did they get all those peanuts? He kept coming back looking like a raspberry. And the poo saga was not at an end. I know, I know! I keep going on about poo, but honestly, the thing I remember most from those days is actually poo. I pinned a cloth on his front with a list of his allergies on so he could go off playing without some well-meaning moron giving him peanuts or biscuits. It didn't work. Either they didn't read it or didn't care, so I swapped it for another one, saying, *If I eat nuts I die!* to see how that did. It didn't. Maybe they didn't notice the rashes under his covering of mud.

Anyhow, I left him with this little group of friends making mud pies – I hope they were mud pies – and headed out, and ended up not far from the barricade, with the tank still parked up next to it, the gun still pointed at the FNA HQ. They'd cleared a space round it, and the commander was sitting there on a camping chair by the tank, smoking weed and drinking a cuppa with a group of people. And among them was Maude.

I didn't go in and try to join them – I'm far too shy for that. They were sitting there like it was a picnic on a sunny day. The commander had a flap-eared cap on, his long legs crossed, cupping his tea in his hands and smiling at Maude. The sun was out, but it was only April, and it wasn't exactly warm. How Maude got in with them so quick, I have no idea. They'd only been here a day, and there she was, sharing a spliff and joking away.

Actually, I can answer that question for you. Maude likes to think she has these big social skills but it's not true. What Maude has is a Body – and boy, does she know how to use it! You should have seen that little group sitting around waiting for their blow on the spliff. Or should I say, just waiting for their blow? They were all sneaking admiring glances at Maude, but they were wasting their time. Know why? Because only one of them was a tank commander. See?

'Negotiations.' Hmm. Prostitution is the correct word, if you want to be polite. I said that to her once, and she wasn't happy.

'You are so full of prejudices, you ought to put them in a bag and sell them down the market,' she told me. Her attitude to it was like, she was some kind of artisan? You know? 'Some people work with their hands, I work with my vagina – get over it!' she said. She had a badge that said that for a while, but she soon got rid of that once the Christian militias started up. You can get thrown off a building for that sort of thing.

She spent quite a bit of time in and around that tank after that. There were three crew, all guys. I didn't like to ask, but somehow she picked up what I thought was going on, and told me it was just her and 'Don', 'having a thing together'. Which I may or may not have believed. And which may or may not have been true. So what? It's none of your business anyway. Or mine, come to that.

8

Anyway. While Maude was off having a fortuitous fling with a tank commander, I was having adventures of my own.

I was sitting with Rowan on the tarp making up a story for him, cos he'd fallen out with some kid and came home crying, when this car came revving not so far away. So I got out to have a look, and guess what? There was an FNA Jeep about twenty or thirty metres away, and guess who was in it? It was only Tariq! Tariq, an old mate of my dad's. Big hairy Pakistani guy. He used to be always round at our house. Him and Dad would sit down and polish off a few bottles of wine and talk politics, and then as soon as Tariq left, my dad would moan about how much wine he'd drunk, and what a big hangover he was going to have the next day. We hadn't seen him for ages and here he was. What about that? In all that chaos.

The Jeep had stopped and there was a crowd growing around him – as soon as people saw someone official-looking they were all over them, trying to find out what was going on, I suppose. I made a beeline for him, shouting and yelling and waving my arms. It was just as well he had the engine off – there were people shouting, and he was in the middle of it with his hands raised, trying to calm them down. He'd just about done and was getting his driver to start up again when I got to the edge of the little crowd.

'TARIQ!' I bellowed.

He turned round and stared at me for a moment, then he shook his head like I was some kind of a circus act. I was still dressed in my gladrags. I'd have been offended if I wasn't so relieved.

'Marti!' he yelled, and he jumped out the Jeep to give me a big hug, while all the Asians stood round looking at us, like, What in the name of Allah is this freakery!

So while useless Maude was having a wank in a tank with a yank (sorry, I couldn't resist it), I was actually being useful making important contacts. I don't call her Rubblehead for nothing.

Not that I imagine there was much actual wanking going on in that tank, mind.

Tariq drove me and Rowan to the FNA command building, in an old pub on the Didsbury Road, (which was very appropriate for a man who used to drink two bottles of wine a night), and gave us tea and sandwiches and cake. Cake! I hadn't had cake for ages. Rowan was gobbling it down like a pig at a trough, and I tried to stop him, but Tariq just waved a hand. 'Let him eat, let him eat, there's plenty more where that came from.' Which was great, except it never came after the little piglet had troughed the first one.

People are like that with little kids. And then as soon as you get to thirteen, they stop thinking you're all cute for gobbling all the cake and they think you're greedy.

Tariq hadn't changed – scoffing cake, drinking beer and

complaining that his wheat allergy was making him bloat. He was quite high up in the FNA, which was a bit of a joke, because the FNA was pro-EU, pro-Western, pro-democracy and pro-free market, and Tariq was a diehard old anticolonial communist. My dad used to call him the last communist in Manchester. He'd been in Bradford for the past couple of months, but they'd recalled him because of all the refugees turning up in Manc. He could speak about eight Asian languages.

Of course he wanted to know what was going on, so I told him a pack of lies. I can admit it to you, can't I? Why? Because I trust you so much? No. But what can *you* do? Sitting there with a book in your hand and thinking you know it all. Well, you don't.

So I told him that Maude had gone off to join the FNA and me and Rowan were trying to head off east to Hull, to get a ferry towards Amsterdam, where my brother was. But now we were stuck! And I was *soooo* worried about my little bruv. And he was a man with contacts . . . an important figure in the local FNA . . . could he help us in any way? Poor Rowan, getting headaches and having nightmares from being under the rubble for three days . . . Boo boo hoo!

Dad's software? Tariq knew all about that, he was on to that pretty quick. No! Tragically lost in the bombing. Yes, all of them. We searched and searched but we never even found them.

I know what you're thinking. You're thinking, what a cow! Deserting her best mate! Dumping her dad's life's work. Well, I'm so sorry, but that's the sort of person I am. Hard as nails. Get used to it. Dumping Maude – you think that was wrong of me? Listen – if she'd got her hands on Tariq first, I'd be on my way south to get my brain turned into a Salvation Army pamphlet and spit-roasted by priests down in the ERAC before you could even spit. I was actually *cursing* myself that I'd brought Rowan along or I'd have said Maude was off with him. He was just another burden as far as I was concerned. Really. Like I say, that's who I am. Live with it, cos it ain't gonna change.

It was going so well. Really well. He was sucking it up. We were actually at the point where he was starting to organise things like a car to carry me east towards Hull, how far he could get us, what the dangers were, that sort of thing. Then he began shaking his head. 'Your dad!' he said. He got all teary, and to be honest so did I. Then . . . 'And your dad's stuff – all that work he did. Gone. What a terrible waste!'

Then he looked at me all crooked and wet-eyed and he said . . . 'He's been seen, you know. Your dad. Yes, he's still alive.'

I froze. I was so shocked! I just stared at him like a beast in the fields. I could hardly speak. Alive? I was so sure he was dead, I knew in my *bones* that he was dead.

I was going, 'But, but, but . . .' as if I wanted him to be dead because . . . because . . . I suppose because I'd got used to it like that.

'But where?' I said.

'The ERAC,' Tariq was saying. He nodded. 'But it's not good news, Marti. He's been rewritten. He's on the other side now. One of them.' He pulled an ugly face. 'Better off dead. If he knew what he'd become . . .'

And I was like, What are you *saying*? That my dad's a Blood? That can't be right. He was always an enemy of the regime! He hated racists, he hated everything they stood for. They could *never* turn him into one of them. He'd die first!

Tariq came around the table and gave me a hug. 'I know how hard this is to accept,' he said. 'I never thought I'd say this, but it would have been better if they'd just killed him, because at least he would have died as himself, instead of living as a monster they invented for their own purposes. But we mustn't give up hope, Marti! The technology they use, it's new, it doesn't work very well. They have him now but that doesn't mean they have him for ever.' He shook his head again. 'It had to be your dad of all people! He was the best hope we had of reversing the rewriting technology. If only that software had got into the right hands, if only we still had it, maybe we could actually get him back.'

I wasn't really taking in what he was saying at that point. I still couldn't believe it. In fact, I refused to believe it, so in the end he pulled up a video he had on his computer.

'Prepare yourself for a nasty shock,' he said.

It was an interview with my dad. And you know, it would have broken my heart to watch it if I'd still had one. He didn't look like he used to, but it was him all right. He'd lost weight, he'd gone grey – even his skin looked grey and he was always quite dark, my dad. He kept squinting and frowning and glaring. He kept losing his temper and shouting, like some kind of nutjob.

But it was what he was saying that really did my head in.

How the Bloods were right. He could see that now. Yes, of

course Black people were inferior to whites. It was obvious when you thought about it.

A load of stuff about how the arts and sciences and industrialisation in Europe was by white people, whereas Black people never did any of that . . .

'All they ever did was bang drums and live in mud huts,' he said.

Tariq put his head in his hands and groaned.

'It doesn't mean we *all* have to become agricultural workers and factory fodder,' my dad was saying. 'Things have moved on. The most able can still rise in a modern society. It doesn't mean Black people are stupid – just that they aren't usually as bright as white people. That their natural urges are less controlled. Less *civilised*. Individual Blacks can move to good positions in society if we behave ourselves and study hard. Some of us have got the talent. It's just that, well, most of us haven't.

'We need to accept our place in the natural order which God created. It's His wish. To each his own station, to each his own estate. We have to learn humility again. All this equality nonsense! Black lives matter, yes, of course they do, but not as much as white ones. Once we submit to our true place in their world, once things get back to where they should be – to where God intended them to be . . . then, who knows? Maybe . . .'

And my dad actually got all teary about this bit.

'Our Heavenly Father might even send His only begotten Son back to Earth and then, brothers and sisters, at the end of days – hallelujah! – Heaven will come to Earth and mankind will live in . . .'

'Turn it off!' I cried. It was unbearable. My dad was always the proudest man who ever walked this Earth. Look what they had done to him!

Tariq terminated the wretched thing.

'Dad would never say that!' I howled. 'It can't be him, it must be some kind of fake.'

Tariq nodded. 'You're right. It's not your dad. It *is* a fake. It's some miserable fiction written by those bastards down in Huntingdon. Your dad is just the medium through which it's played. I'm so sorry, Marti. I'm so, so sorry.'

I felt like my whole world had been blown away. I loved my dad so much! I loved my mum, too. Look, I stayed in Manchester for her – there was no other reason. But me and my dad – we had a special connection. We were like . . . I don't know how to say it. We were like it should be between a parent and their child.

Let me tell you about my dad.

His skin is beautiful – the colour of old pine. I used to tell him he was the colour of antique furniture, and he would say that was because he *was* an antique. He's handsome. His hair's in neat little dreads, some of them going grey, and he has a high, wide forehead, and inside that is his marvellous brain. You think I'm just saying that, but you have no idea how clever my dad is. He is *so* clever! He used to tip his head back to look at you when he was talking, following his thread, and then you'd see his eyes go off into the distance, because he'd forget who he was talking to. He'd go off into some theoretical stuff

I never could follow, but he always came back and remembered who he was talking to, and translated himself into simple things I could understand. Yes, he was away a lot, but he was never distant, he was never patronising, he always engaged with you. And yes, he had a hard time accepting me for who and what I am, and yes, that did change things between us a bit. But he never stopped loving me and trying to help me. And he was fun – so much fun! We were always laughing together, I think he lived to talk and to laugh. In many ways, he was the best dad in the world, which is why I hated him when he went away so much and left me with my crazy mum.

He has the most beautiful fingers – long, neat active fingers, tapering towards the end. Look! Like this. I have his fingers. They're my best feature. And he always looked good, whether he dressed in his suit or jeans and trainers. My dad looked so good, even in his *pyjamas*, he still looked good. He loved me and I loved him. And he was still alive. Still alive. But . . .

Tariq was going on about how there was still hope, how we could still save him, how they had their best people working on how to gain control of the mainframe at Huntingdon and put all the rewriting they did there into reverse, to find a way to undo it to give them themselves back.

'Because they can't get rid of your old self without completely destroying your mind,' he said. 'If they'd done that to him, all he'd be doing is grinning like a zombie and praising the Lord. If they want you to talk like he does, they have to just block off your access to your old personality, not destroy it. Your dad is still in there somewhere, hidden inside his brain, cut off from his own mind. If only his work had survived, we could have got him back. Such a shame! But other people are working on this as well . . .'

On he rattled. And . . . I couldn't do it, could I? *My dad's work*. Think about it. Tariq was telling me that my phone could actually save him. I'm not a good person. I do bad things. I could let Maude down, I could let Rowan down. But not my dad. I could never let my dad down.

I started crying properly then, and Tariq came to comfort me. I was saying, 'What have I done, what have I done?'

And he was saying, 'You mustn't blame yourself, Marti, you did your best, there's nothing anyone could have done, it's this bloody war.'

And I was saying, 'No, you don't understand, it really is my fault.'

And I told him the truth.

Tariq looked utterly astonished. He listened carefully to it all and then he said, 'And Maude?'

'Still at the camp,' I sniffed. I had my head down. I couldn't look him in the face. It's so hard when you get caught out.

He went round behind his desk and sat down.

'So, when did you become such a little shit, Marti?' he said quietly. 'Lying about the software that so many people depend on. Dumping your friends? You and Maude are practically sisters.' The bastard was actually leaking tears. 'You weren't like this when you were young. Is it the war? Is this the way young people are turning out? Because if they are,' he said, 'we have no hope left.'

'It's the war,' I told him. 'I'm not like this really.' Although I knew I was. I was so ashamed. Even he was embarrassed. That's how bad it was. He was right of course. There *was* no hope. But not because of my generation. Because of *his!* His lot brought us to this, brought *me* to this. That's the truth, isn't it?

I wish I'd thought to say it at the time, but I couldn't even speak. All I could do was sit there and bend my head and watch the tears dripping off the end of my nose onto my lap. I was so ashamed. Being a bad person is much easier if no one ever finds out about it.

9

Yes, I was given a hard time by Tariq about trying to dump Maude and lying about the phone, which I suppose I deserved. Not that Maude seemed to care all that much. It was hard to make her out sometimes. Sometimes it was like she'd lay down her life for me, whereas I wouldn't've given up a packet of bread rolls for her. But she always took it on the chin. She'd get cross for about ten minutes, then calm down and we'd be mates again. If that were me, I'd never speak to her again.

But all that was besides the point. The point was – my dad was alive! That changed everything. Like I say, I'm hard and cold, a heartless bitch. But I wasn't always like this. I was never exactly what you'd call a sweet kid – people like me don't get away with sweet. But I did love someone and that person was my dad. Yes, I loved my dad. It used to break my heart when he went away. Really, it killed me over and over again. And he loved me back. He did. He *adored* me. My mum always used to say how much he adored me. When I was a baby, as soon as I was born, he plucked me up off her breast and wouldn't give me back until the midwife told him off. She told me that story a hundred times. I used to make her say it two or three times in a row, I loved it so much.

In the end, I did get a bit more used to him going away. He

73

used to talk to me about how it would be if anything happened to him, so I suppose I must have been preparing for it because when finally he did disappear, I hardly cared. Funny, eh? I never felt a thing.

But now that he was back – *bam!* I was . . . I don't know what I was. I was delighted, I was dancing! I was angry, furious with him for going away and then furious with him again for coming back into my life like this, in a way that stopped my ideas of escape dead in their tracks. I was ashamed. I was jubilant! No way could I abandon my dad! No way.

I let Maude and Tariq tell me off for being mean – why should I care what they think? – and then I went outside and I found a big lump of mud and I smashed it up, I punched it and I kicked it and I gouged its eyes out. I wished it had been a baby I was doing it to, that's how angry I was. Because now I was actually going to *have* to do it. Go to the ERAC, after all. You see? That's how I am. I could happily do over Rowan, eat his sweets, steal his blanket, leave him out for the dogs and still have a good night's sleep. I could sell Maude to a travelling brothel and eat out on the proceeds for a week and it wouldn't have bothered me one bit. But I could never, ever leave my dad to be a racist bastard working for the Bloods. It was impossible for me.

It was like a little door creaked open in my heart. And who needs an open heart in a war zone? I'd spent ages keeping it shut and now some bastard had got a lever and started wrenching it open. That bastard was my dad. Hearts are for Amsterdam and falling in love and having friends and people around you who don't disappear. Not for here – not here, of all places!

It gave me *hope*. I've never been so furious about anything in my life.

Of course, if my stupid dad hadn't been so ridiculously clever, we'd have been able to copy the software, or zap it over the internet or something easy like that. But no. He was so paranoid about the Bloods getting their hands on it, he had a virus in it so as soon as it was copied, it self-destructed. The phone had to be delivered in person and the software uploaded into the mainframe and nothing else would do. But none of that meant that I'd given up on my dreams. I was already hatching a plan, a plan that meant I wasn't going to have to go down south actually *in person*. If I gave the phone to Tariq, he could get it delivered for us. Yes, it had to be delivered in person. But not necessarily by me. I know Maude had failed to get the FNA to deal with it, but now we had Tariq on our side. When Maude asked them, it was just some daft tart trying to do a favour for a crazy dead black guy. But Tariq was different. He *knew* my dad was a genius. AND he was an officer or whatever it is they have in the FNA. It sounded like 'case solved' to me.

I oiled him up. He was a big man, a strong man. A man with authority. He'd stand a much better chance of bringing my dad's work to life than two stupid kids . . . You know the sort of thing. But he just looked at me as if I was something that dripped out of the dog's bottom.

That's right. He had my number.

'Even if I didn't have responsibilities here in the north, I couldn't do it,' he said. Like everyone else, he had problems of his own – his own family. They'd gone to visit people in

Birmingham a couple of months ago – just in time for the Bloods to come storming in. He'd heard nothing from them since.

'They might be on the move,' he said. 'My best hope is to stay up here to see if they turn up with the other refugees.'

I didn't say anything, but it didn't sound like much of a hope to me. You don't get much mobile coverage these days, but you do get some from time to time. Surely he'd have heard from them by now if they were still alive and free.

Maude wasn't quite so delicate about it as I was.

'That long and you haven't heard from them? F**k that,' she said. 'If they're not dead, they're in the ERAC by now.' She waggled the phone with the software on it in his face. 'So it may be that this baby is your best hope of getting them back. Come with us, Tariq.'

The poor guy had gone grey, but he still shook his head.

'Do you think I haven't thought of that? I had word that they got robbed, so they may have no phones. I was always on at them to memorise my number in case of this sort of thing, but none of them ever did. My best information is that they started off walking north. Sorry, I can't do it. If I don't find them up here, maybe I'll come after you, but that won't be for a while. You're going to have to do it yourselves.'

'There's bigger things at stake than your own family here,' said Maude, the stuck-up bitch.

'I know. I know I should be helping get that software to those poor bastards in the ERAC, but what can you do? I'm as bad as Marti. Can't try to save the rest of the world while there's even a tiny chance to save my own people first.'

'It's not good, but don't compare yourself to Marti, you're not that bad,' said Maude, which I think was her effort to try and comfort him.

So that was it. If we wanted to rescue my dad, we had to do it ourselves. But Tariq did help us a bit. It took him three or four days, but he came up with the goods in the end. A motorbike! Come on, how cool is that? Maude was a biker, we used to go everywhere on her old Suzuki 250 until someone nicked it. You got to love a bike. Apart from being terminally cool, it's nifty. You can go off-road, you can weave between the gaps on a bike. You can dodge bullets. It was a battle-scarred old thing they came up with for us, an old Honda, but the engine was good and the tank was full. If we got a good run, we could be down there in a day. Depending on the roads, of course. And the roadblocks. And the kidnappers, snipers, etc. Etc, etc, etc.

Given that he was willing to let two innocent young girls – one of them a walking bundle of visible corruption – ride into the Valley of Death, Tariq did his best for us. He got us in touch with one of the lead guys in the resistance down around Huntingdon and told him we were coming.

'Bobby Rose. I used to know him from when we were bringing a case against the police for brutality back in the day,' he said. 'Brilliant young lawyer then, but of course there's no need for lawyers now as there's no law. He's a c**t. But he's a brilliant leader.'

Great. Better and better.

'Make sure you give the phone to him personally. There's all sorts of people would like to get their hands on that software down there. Bobby's an arrogant bastard, but he has the hardware to use it and he'll do anything to get at the Bloods. He has family of his own in that facility. You can rely on him to give it a proper go.'

As I say, the way it worked, the Bloods used these shortwave drones at night to block your existing memories, then they implanted your mind with their poisonous drivel. That was my dad's master stroke, you see – using the drones to reverse programme the mainframe to cut out the block and give the people their precious memories back. The trouble is, we couldn't be sure he'd actually done it. And if he had done it, we didn't know if it still worked with whatever upgrades the Bloods had put into their system. So it was all a pretty long shot.

Maude was willing to do it for the sake of the fight. And me? My dad was in there. And wouldn't it be great if I could use his own software to give him back his mind? I don't suppose he even remembered who I was right now . . .

'Once I get my family somewhere safe, I'll try to join you,' Tariq told us.

'We won't keep our fingers crossed,' I said, and the poor old guy bent his bald head. I only meant that we weren't going to depend on him, that I knew his family came first. I was trying to be nice, but I guess it didn't come across like that, because later, after he'd gone, I was bending over to wipe Rowan's nose and Maude gave me the most enormous kick up the arse.

'What was that for?' I said.

'For being mean to Tariq,' she said. I didn't even bother explaining to her. Once some people get an idea about you in their heads there's no shifting it, especially if they don't get that

78

many ideas. Especially if they spent too long lying around with a house on top of their heads. Know what I mean?

I was furious though. In front of Rowan, too. She was a tough cookie, Maude – she had big meaty thighs so she could dole out a kick. I had her when it came to the upper body strength, though. I could have broken that pretty little nose of hers easy, if I got a punch in. But she had the edge on me, because while she was as fearless as a dragon, I'm a piece of chickenshit. I can't help it – it's the way I am. If ever I get into a fight, the other guy is always thinking about how much it would hurt me to break my nose for me. Trouble is, that's all I can think about as well.

There was the usual debate about which way to go. The main roads might be quicker but there were more likely to be refugees and troop movements. Roadblocks and stuff can slow you to a standstill, as we'd just seen. On the other hand, on the little roads across the Peaks, there was more danger of ambush. It was mainly the little militias we had to worry about there. As I said, the Bloods were shooting up the west side of the country like a rash but they were taking their time on the east side. They'd taken Northampton a few weeks ago and stopped there. The ERAC lay in their territory, and we were going to have to go underground when we got down there – if we got there. Let's face it, there was no way I was going to go into Blood territory in broad daylight and come out in one piece.

In the end, we decided to go through the Peak District on the small roads, away from the towns and bigger villages – across to Nottingham, and then straight down to Huntingdon.

Tariq – bless him! – was going to give us and the bike a lift in a truck to Buxton, and we'd set off from there.

'Don't stop, don't talk to anyone, go cross country. Do whatever it takes,' he said. 'The further south you go, the more likely you are to come across the Bloods. And you must stay out of their hands at all costs,' Tariq told us. Told *us*, but he was looking at me.

'I'll look after her,' said Maude, but Tariq shook his head.

'If they get her down south, they'll kill her. And they'll make a mess doing it.'

Maude licked her lips.

'What about me?' she asked.

Tariq tipped his head. 'Rape, then the ERAC,' he said.

'Huh, what they'd do to me would make rape look like a hot date with Michael Bublé,' I told her. Which was meant to be a joke – just trying to lighten the mood. But they both looked at me like I just did a poo on the kitchen table.

'It's not a competition, Marti,' said Tariq.

'She has white cis privilege, which means I have black queer disadvantage,' I said. 'It's not much, but it's mine and I'm hanging on to it.' Which made Tariq laugh and he high-fived me.

'You're a selfish little bitch but at least you have a sense of humour,' he chuckled. But as far as I was concerned, I was only telling the truth. I always do.

10

Finally! We'd left Fallowfield over a week ago and so far we'd done about two miles down the road. But now we were really off – in a truck! We were in Buxton within a few hours. Can you believe that? Suddenly – boom! And awaaaaaaaay!

We spent the night all nice and cosy in a safe house, with a cooked dinner. Buxton, yeah – it was AMAZING. Just a few hours away, and there was no fighting, the buildings were all standing, the roads were clear. There was wi-fi! And data! All the NFA people there were boasting about how great Buxton was, how well everyone got on together.

'It's live and let live here,' one of them said. They were like, It could never happen here. 'People here get on too well together.'

'Everyone says that – until it happens,' said Tariq, the miserable old miserablist. 'They'll be here, same as everywhere, hiding away – the racists, the terrorists, the Bloods, the fascists. Once they get a chance, they'll be out setting fire to people's homes and all the rest of it – you'll see.'

I didn't want to hear it. I took myself to my room – yeah, I had a whole room to myself – so I could spend my time texting my mates, who had fled all over the world and were sitting safe on their pretty powdered bottoms going, Oh, look, isn't it just DREADFUL what's happening back home, from the safety of

New York or Amsterdam or Glasgow or whatever. I was sooo jealous!

I didn't get very far with it though, because Rowan came in and wanted me to go for a walk with him and Maude, the little pest. But I went anyway.

It was bliss. Shops. You know? People walking up and down in fashionable clothes. It was like the old days! The war just hadn't got to Buxton. I mean, there were shortages, but that was about it. We were taking selfies standing next to a shop, or in a shop buying something, or going over a zebra crossing to look at another shop. Rowan was in absolute heaven because he'd never done *any* of those things, ever. All he knew was bomb sites and snipers. Just walking down the street was like this big treat for him. Poor little thing thought he was in Disneyland or something. Me and Maude had loads of fun spotting things to show him. Traffic lights! He spent five minutes watching traffic lights going on and off. Then we found him a neon display. That sort of thing.

We had ice cream in a cafe. I found one of those rides for little ones outside a shop, a reindeer sleigh, and put some money in so he could have a go. I bought him a toy tank and a doll. He didn't really want the doll, but in these days of equal rights I thought it was only right.

Yes, me and Rowan were kindred spirits there for a few hours, but Maude started being a misery. She was like, Shops, huh. So what? Like it was all beneath her. Then she had to skip off to do some deal – she was trying to get one of the FNA blokes to come along with us. I didn't ask what kind of 'deal' she was trying to strike. Let's face it, Maude's a girl with only one treasure on her person – *in* her person, I should say – but it's the gift that keeps on giving.

'Safety in numbers,' she said. I nearly suggested that if she stayed here long enough, she could recruit a whole battalion, but I kept my mouth shut, which is more than you can say for Maude, I bet.

Off she went, taking our money with her. Well, you know what? I had some of my own, money she knew nothing about, so we really went off on the spend with her out of the way. I bought Rowan some clothes and let him pay for them. I took a great picture of him looking over his shoulder and smiling like a gangster as he hands over the money. All he had were his tattered old T-shirts and sweatshirts and stuff. It cost a bomb. I got myself a new handbag, too. It cost as much as all Rowan's stuff put together, but I'm a fashionable young woman and he's just a smudge on the face of the Earth. It wasn't fair him getting everything.

So – yeah! No one can say I didn't treat my little bro right sometimes. I gave him the time of his life, then we went back and I lay on my bed and texted my mates and played a game or two, until Maude came in waving the shoes and stuff I'd bought him and demanding where did these come from, do you think we're made of money, you idiot, Martina?

'I have money of my own,' I told her. Then she went bonkers and we had a fight, which she won and got her hands on my bag and found my money, which made me wail like a lost soul.

'YOU don't have money, WE have money, you tight cow,' she yelled. 'What's mine is yours—'

'And what's mine is mine as well,' I finished off for her. So then I grabbed hold of Rowan and wept all over him and told him that nasty Maude was stealing my things and making me cry.

'Jesus, Marti, you're a piece of work, you're a f*****g piece of work,' she hissed. She stormed out and threw the money back at me. Well, she can share what she likes. She does it all the time. But what's mine stays mine. That's all there is to it.

Anyway. Like I say, hand it to Maude, she'd get cross and then it'd all be over by the next day. She put things into boxes in her head, she must have had a head like a filing cabinet, the way she tucked stuff away. Me, my head is like a crap handbag. Everything's tumbling around in there. The top of the lipstick has come off, the compact has burst. You know? It's a mess.

So I got up the next day and had a hot shower! It had been so long since I had one of those. They fed us eggs and toast and stuff. Really, really nice. Then we got on the bike, Maude in front driving – I was planning on having a go at that later on – Rowan in the middle and me on the back. And off we went! Yeah! Fast and sweet, swerving through the traffic, out onto the roads and – *bang!* Off on the main road like a rocket, all three of us shouting into the wind like idiots. It felt so, so, so, so good. I felt almost happy.

11

As we were whizzing along, I put my earphones in and listened to my daily dose of tunes on my secret phone, which had now become a public phone. After a campaign of consistent nagging, Maude had finally given it back to me, even though it had the only copy of dad's software on it. I had sentimental feelings about that phone – it was the only thing I owned which came from my dad. Maude was pretty reluctant, but she knew me well enough to know that where my dad was involved, that was the one area where I was to be trusted.

I had Marvin Gaye on, because I'd found out something interesting about him while I was lying on my bed faffing about on the internet for the first time in years. He was a cross-dresser. How about that? Who knew? I always supposed my dad put him on the playlist because, well, partly because he was Black but also because of 'What's Going On'. But maybe it was because he was just so far out there, gender politics-wise. My dad was pretty good on that sort of stuff once he got his head round it.

It wasn't all my dad's music on that phone, he'd put some of my mum's favourite stuff on it too, stuff from when she was young – way before my time, because by the time I knew her she mainly listened to my dad's music for some reason. Stuff like the Chemical Brothers or Daft Punk. It was good stuff, some of it, but I think you need to be on Es to get the most out of that sort of music. I listened to some of that, too, as we went along, in honour of my mum.

It was a lovely sunny day, big fluffy white clouds. Dappled light. The leaves on the trees were coming out so everything was dusted green on that lovely spring day. There were big pink cherry trees scattered about the villages and towns like clouds. We got out of Buxton soon enough and then we were into the countryside proper, climbing up the hills of the Peaks.

I remembered it, sort of. It felt like that, anyway. My mum and dad used to take me up there when I was small, just us three, back before the war. It felt like my childhood up there. Manchester was where I really grew up, of course, but the fighting had kind of ruined it for me. So I soaked this up, because who knew how long before this would disappear, too? And I listened to the music on my earphones, and I thought about my mum.

She was a useless kind of person to have about when there's a war on, but if it had been peace time she'd have been pretty good as a mum, I reckon. She looked after me very well when I was small. She carried on trying afterwards, but it was too late by then. She begged me to look after my education, but I never listened to her, which is why I only have my natural wits to get me through. And she never stopped nagging, which I suppose is a kind of love, isn't it? Annoying love. She kept trying. A few months before she died, she decided my hair was a mess and that she was going to braid it for me. I used to get a friend of mine to braid it before her family left town, so I was quite pleased, because Mum used to make some lovely stuff – she was always a big one for cookery, for instance, and she could make these really fiddly little things, icing on cakes, stuffed vegetables, that sort of thing. So I had high hopes.

But she turned out to be hopeless at braiding hair! It was unbelievable – I looked like some crazy person had been trying to invent a new language on my head. It was dreadful. I was all polite to her and said thank you very much, that's great, thanks, Mum. She was frowning at it and saying, I'll get better than that, Marti, I'll get better than that. But she never did. Every time it was crap.

Maude was on at me to keep letting her, so's she'd be happy she was doing something for me. 'She just wants to be helpful, Marti, that's all. She just wants to be useful.'

Well, yes, don't we all? But she wasn't. I couldn't go about looking like that! So instead I offered to swap foot massages and pedicures with her. Which I also regretted. I know, I know – I'm being a moaner and I hate moaners! But you don't know my mum. Actually, although I was scared she was going to cut me, she did OK, did a good job on the pedicures. I had pretty good, well-cared for tootsies after that for a while. But I had to do hers as well, and what I hadn't realised was she had toenails like a mountain goat! Great horny things that would have been more use for trotting up and down the mountainside than walking up and down Victoria Grove. Like hooves.

'I know!' hissed Maude when I pointed it out. 'I wondered if you'd seen them when you volunteered.'

See? Even Maude thought like that. But I had to keep doing

it, although it nearly took my eye out a few times. Mum claimed it was some sort of fungal thing, so we got some treatment from a bombed-out chemist and I actually think we were making some kind of progress when that bomb came and cured her nails, along with a whole lot else.

My memories made me cry, sitting on the back of the bike, listening to my mum's dance tunes. My tears blew away in the wind behind me. My poor mum. She was the one who accepted me first. My dad kept saying, It's just a phase, it's just a phase, and she gave him a hard time until he came round. She knew how to love, but I don't know what else she knew. She taught me one thing though. In this world, love is not enough, despite everything they say in the songs.

Once we got into the country Maude really opened up the bike. We were swooping around the corners, me and Rowan glued to her, arms round her waist. We went so fast! I didn't even care although I'm an utter scaredy-cat. We swooped, we soared, we flew, roaring along the valleys and up the hills, and the countryside just opened up before us.

Our first stop was a tiny little village called Monyash, where we were supposed to drop off a couple of parcels from the FNA guys in Buxton. It was, I dunno, maybe half an hour away. Nothing really. Monyash was a secret supply store for the local FNA.

It was such a pretty little village as we rode down the hill towards it. It was tiny – a few houses, some of 'em quite big though, all built with this honey-coloured stone. A church spire pointing up to the sky. There were some tall trees around it, dappled green with sunlight. Cows in the field. It was so pretty, Maude stopped at the crest of the hill so we could get a proper look. It was like, your eyes were parched dry from months of looking at rubble and frightened people, and this was a long cool drink of beautifulness. We just waited and soaked it up for a few minutes, then she pushed off and we swept down the hill, the engine just ticking over, past a farmhouse and barn and into the village itself.

It was all very still. There was a smell like an old bonfire. That was the first thing. I made to get off, but Maude put her hand on my arm.

'Just a mo,' she said.

We were on the village green, bright green and mown not long before. There was a cross in the middle of it, and a pond to one side. There was a rookery there, with the rooks cawing. There were other black birds at the edge of the pond, looking across at us, and a couple sitting on the cross.

Maude drove over to the pond and then we saw it. That cross, it wasn't a cross, it was just a pointed stone, the war memorial. The cross pieces were arms, tied to a plank. Someone had been crucified on it.

We both froze. Then our eyes started working and we saw. There were more bodies in the mud around the pond. The crows were pecking at them.

'Go go go!' I hissed. But the silly cow didn't. She drove over towards the church. I was crapping myself. I leaned against Rowan, put my arms round Maude's waist and closed my eyes. 'Maude, Maude, just get us out of here,' I begged.

'What, Marti, what?' Rowan was going, but neither of us answered.

That smell of charred wood was getting stronger but she went on, right up to the church door. I mean, they could have been anywhere, the people who did it. You could see then that the church roof was gone. How had we missed that when we were looking down from the hill? All we wanted to see was beautifulness, that's why. The windows all had black above them like scary eyebrows.

Maude got off the bike and took her gun out. The door was scorched black in the middle. She shoved at it with her foot, but it was locked so it didn't open. But it crunched under her boot. She glanced over to me. I mean, that was a good thick church door. She stood back and gave it few good hard kicks, which made me die of fright – the noise she made! Anyone could hear it! – and the door caved in. It had been burned from the inside, you see, so the outside just looked like darkened wood, but behind that it was all charcoal.

She stood back and gave it a few more hefty kicks that knocked a hole in it, and we peered in.

Black everywhere. Charcoal. The stink of charred wood and burning, and . . . other burnt things. There was a pile of those other burnt things heaped up by the door and it took me a moment, just a moment, to work out what it was. You know?

Maude jumped back, I jumped back. Christ! That was enough even for her. She leaped back on the bike double quick, drove us as fast as she could, fast, fast, fast, as fast as she could away. We were just getting out of it when someone opened fire on us . . . *rata-tatat-a-tat-atat!* There was a thud, the bike swerved, but we straightened up and we were away again. Fast as you like!

I thought, So much for beautiful. Where does beautiful get you? That little place, that pretty little place, it did my head in. It wasn't as though there were any fighters there. It was just because they supported the wrong side that all those people got killed like that. Some of those shapes by the door were only small. They'd locked them in the church behind that big door and set fire to it. All those people . . . children . . . old people . . . everyone.

Rowan and I were clutching hold of Maude and she was clutching the bike, and we were going way too fast. After a bit I saw there was blood on me but I couldn't work out where it was from. I patted myself but I seemed OK. Then the smell of petrol. There was a stream of it flowing out of the tank and I didn't want us to stop yet, we weren't far enough away, so I leaned around Rowan and I put my finger in the hole. Then I realised there was an exit hole on the other side of the tank, so I put my finger in that hole too.

Then I saw that Rowan's hand was bleeding – that was the blood, see – and he only had half a finger on one hand. I tried to press my finger on the stump to stop the bleeding, but then the petrol was coming out again, so I made Maude pull over.

She cut the engine and got off. I was still straddling the bike with my finger in the holes. She went crazy when she saw that Rowan was bleeding. 'Why didn't you tell me, why didn't you tell me?' she shouted, and started ripping up her shirt for a tourniquet. Rowan, who hadn't made a sound all the way through this, suddenly started screaming his head off and fighting her and shouting, 'Marti, Marti, Marti!' and holding his arms out to me. Which was so confusing and annoying. He never had any time for me and I never had any time for him up till then.

Maude handed him over to me and watched while I tried to tie a knot round his finger to stop the bleeding.

'It must be because you've been looking after him for the past few days,' she said in a hurt voice.

'Yeah, you were in the tank with the yank. Don't worry, I won't be doing it again,' I told her.

But it wasn't over yet. Before you knew it, there were engines coming towards us. I slapped my hand over his screaming little mouth and made a dash for the hedgerow. Maude tried to get the bike, but it fell over so she tried to drag it. But it caught on something and it weighed a tonne anyway so she had to leave it on its side with the petrol glugging out of it, stinking the place up, and ran to hide next to me.

A Land Rover went past. White folk in it. White-on-white atrocities here in the pretty old Peaks. They went gliding past, not in a hurry, not bothering much, like an old dog checking that whoever it had scared off was gone. Luckily, the bike was half hidden in the long dry grass from last year and they missed it. Once they were past, Maude dashed out and got the bike behind the hedge with us. Stood it upright behind the hedge, but God knows how much petrol we'd lost.

'You silly bint,' I told her.

Rowan had wet himself by now which meant that he'd wet me as well because he'd been sitting on my lap, which was utterly disgusting. Then I had to sit there very still with the screaming wetter on my lap while Maude bandaged his hand properly. First aider, see? Woman of many parts.

Then the car came back, and we were sitting in that hedge holding our breath and pooing ourselves because we'd realised by now that there was a petrol trail along the road that stopped where we'd pulled over. But these guys, they were all very good at locking families in a church and setting fire to it, but they obviously weren't good at much else because they utterly failed to notice anything.

And then we had to sit in that hedge quaking for ages, afraid to start the engine, till we felt safe to carry on.

Inside that church. That was a sight you never want to see because once you have you can never unsee it. I saw it every day for a while, until worse things happened that I can never forget, ever, no matter what happens. Then being scared by the nutjobs that did it, then being wet by Rowan. And then to cap it all, little Rowan transferring his replacement Mumsie allegiance from Maude to me. How did that happen? I didn't even like him.

It didn't last long, fortunately. Sitting in that hedge with my hand wrapped around his face to stop him screaming was a good start. He wasn't so keen on me after that. I gave him a few hard pinches on the bike as well, which put him right off me. It was for his own good. Look, you know something about me by now. Less than you think, but some. Do I seem like the motherly sort? I don't think so.

We bunged up the tank with some bits of stick off the hedgerow and paper and wrappers and a T-shirt (one of Maude's of course.) I had Vaseline in my make-up bag and we tried to seal it with that, not very successfully. And off we went. Me pushing the bike very quietly at first, with Maude a hundred metres behind keeping an eye out for nutjobs. Then after about half a mile we got on it – very slowly and quietly to start with, then a bit faster – then she opened up the throttle and off we went, fast, fast, fast – away from that evil place.

So we got away, but we'd lost so much fuel there was no way we were going to get all the way to Nottingham. It wasn't an utter disaster because the guys in Buxton had given us a list of safe houses in Matlock. It was touch and go if we'd make it that far, but we got there in the end. We had a little trouble finding the safe house, it wasn't obvious, but I suppose that's the point. It was tucked away in a little row of terraces overlooking some allotments.

I was a mess, but Maude had held it together the whole way, really cool – so I thought anyway, but as soon as she got off the bike she started to cry and once we were inside she just flung her arms around one of the FNA guys and sobbed into his neck.

The guy looked horrified. 'What happen, what happen?' he kept saying, but she couldn't speak. One of them came to me, touched me on the arm and asked if I was OK.

'Yeah, I'm OK,' I said. 'You could have a look at my brother, though.'

They were horrified when I told them about the massacre. It was a big thing, one of the worst things that had ever happened, because it was families and kiddies and babies and old people. You know? It was a big brutal step up in the violence. Some of the guys there knew those people.

Then they all went into a panic in case the people there had given away the FNA places in Matlock, so suddenly everyone was charging around, moving house. I wasn't sure they needed to do that at first because the massacre had clearly happened a few days ago and they were still there, still alive. You know? But really they had to move because, well, how can you tell?

So we didn't have nearly such a good night in Matlock as we'd had in Buxton. But that's life, I guess.

12

It won't be a surprise to you to know that I used to get bullied at school. You know the ones – the cool, sporty ones who stick together and everyone wants to be like them? And they *want* everyone to be like them and if you're not, it's like some sort of insult? Well, *I* didn't want to be like them. I thought I was the cool one and they were just jealous. They hated that.

'What the f**k do you think you look like?' they used to say to me.

And I used to look them up and down, and say, 'Are you kidding me?' And then they used to hit me.

'The thing about those kids is, they think they're so great, but you know what? This is *it* for them,' my dad said, when I went back home crying. 'As soon as they leave school, they're on their way down. It's the geeks, the queers, the freaks, the gays, the Blacks and the monsters who are going to inherit the Earth, I promise you. None of *them* will ever amount to anything.'

Which was hopelessly wrong, obviously. It's the sporty, well-dressed bigots who rule the world now and people like me who are in danger of extinction. But still, it was a nice thought.

'It's downhill all the way for you guys now,' I told them the next day. And then I got hit again. But I never stopped saying it, and it never stopped driving them mad, which convinced me that it was true, of course.

So there was this time I got kept back after school because these kids had been bullying me in the playground. The teacher, Mr Siddon he was called, he came out and caught them kicking me on the ground. So he asked them what I'd done to deserve it and they said, 'He said we'd peaked, Sir.'

So guess who got into trouble? Me, of course!

'Marti,' he said afterwards. 'Marti, I'm afraid that you are a deeply flawed character.'

Deeply flawed? You know? But of course what I heard wasn't 'deeply flawed', it was deeply *floored*. So I was looking around thinking, what is he on about? *Deeply floored.* I even looked down at my shoes to see if I was standing in a hole or something.

Then off he went, about how provocative I was, and about my attitude, and how I needed to fit in better and give people their space instead of shoving my differences in their faces.

So I went home and told my mum and dad. My mum thought it was hilarious and laughed like a drain being emptied. But Dad – he was furious. In fact he was incandescent. He went straight down to that school, and you know what he did for me, my dad? He had a go at that teacher, and he recorded the whole thing on his phone! How cool is that? So I could play it back and listen to what he thought of the guy.

It was great. 'This school is a hotbed of bullying and intolerance that goes all the way to the top,' my dad said. 'Yes – I'm talking about the staff, Mr Siddon. I'm talking about *you*.'

And Siddon was spluttering and coughing. Boy, had he got it wrong, picking on a kid whose dad was *my* dad!

'A child gets bullied and that child gets into trouble with the *staff*?' said my dad. 'What about the actual *bullies*? What happened to them? Did you give them a medal? What I want to know, Mr Siddon, is why you're picking on my daughter yourself? Why are *you* bullying her? Is it because that's your nature? Is it because you're frightened of these boys? Do they have something on you? Or is it just because you're just lazy and bad at your job. Well? Tell me. Which is it?'

And so on.

Dad told me not to tell Siddon I'd heard the whole thing, but the next time I spoke to Siddon I couldn't resist dropping in the odd phrase, like . . . 'Think again,' which was one of my dad's phrases that he used all the time. Or, 'Pigs may fly but prejudice never can,' which was another one. And which I've never understood, by the way, because it's not even remotely true. I've noticed that about a lot of proverbs and sayings. They sound like they're true. People say them like they're being wise but as soon as you think about it you realise what bullshit it really is.

I know what you're saying. You're saying, Why are you telling me this? What's this got to do with anything? I'm telling you so that you know what kind of a dad I had. I had *that* kind of dad. That incident is one of many. So that you know why I adored him so much. He was my hero. Used to be, anyway – before he abandoned his family to go away and fight the cause and get himself turned into a racist fool.

I tried to ring his phone when we were in Buxton and again in Matlock. It was stupid, really. It would break my heart to hear him go on the way he did in that video. Also I was scared that he'd turn out to be dead after all, because in a war zone, being alive can be a very temporary thing. And I was scared that if he was alive and not himself any more, he'd try to talk me round to his way of thinking. What if I started agreeing with him, just because he was my dad? See, when that teacher said I was deeply flawed, actually . . . he was right. I am actually a walking mass of deep flaws, as you may have noticed.

But he never picked up. I guess they'd taken his phone off him or maybe he'd managed to destroy it before he got caught. Who knows – anything could be true now that they can change you into whoever they want. Maybe he knew that I was on my way, so that he could hand me over to the Bloods. Maybe . . .

People often say about someone they used to be close to, that they don't know them any more. It was never as true as it was for me and my dad. Who was he now? And – how cool would it be if my phone could give him back to me. How cool? Cooler than all the fashion labels in the world. Cooler than Amsterdam, I hear you say? Yeah, really. Even cooler than that.

I rang my bruv in Amsterdam, too. You have to keep your options open. No answer there either. I guess he was too busy frolicking with all those virgins in Paradise. Lucky guy.

13

We spent a day hanging around with Rowan's finger, but events were moving faster than we were. The Bloods were on the move, occupying towns and villages, putting up roadblocks, rooting out anyone opposed to them. The longer we left it, the harder it was going to be to get down south, let alone back up to Hull and Amsterdam, city of my dreams. I was prepared to put my life on hold to try to save my dad, but after that, I was sticking to plan A. I'd be off to Hull before you could cough. I wanted to spend my war years whooping it up in the sex capital of Europe, not languishing in a prison camp, thank you very much.

I kept nagging to go, but kids always come first, never mind whether they deserve it or not. And then, if you argue against it, it's like you're some kind of monster. To make it worse, the Nottingham guys actually offered to take him off our hands! They knew a charity that would take him in.

'Pretty little kid like that,' one of them said. 'People'd pay a lot of money for a kid like that.'

'Even with half a finger missing!' I said. No one laughed.

'The important thing is,' this bloke said, 'it'd be *safer* for him. He'd have a good life. If you loved him, that's what you'd do. If I had a baby brother,' he said wistfully, 'I'd do it for him. Really. It's the best thing.'

As far as I was concerned, it was a no-brainer. No kid to look after? Money? Safe place for said kid? What are we waiting for? But Maude was dead to our appeals.

'Your own brother,' she said to me. She was always saying that.

'It's for his *own good*,' I said.

'Like pinching him on his side was for his own good?' she said. Typical. The little wretch had snitched on me!

She had a real rant about it. How people couldn't be trusted when money was involved. How there was no guarantee that Rowan was going to go to a good home. 'It could be some awful place. Like, slavery. Or some pervy thing. And you,' she said, 'you want to risk that for *your own baby brother*!' And – this is the killer – 'And anyway, Marti, you promised Mum!'

She was always saying that. It was true, me and Maude, we both made that promise. When Dad disappeared, Mum made us promise that if anything ever happened to her, we'd all stick together. I guess the difference between me and Maude was, that while I promised it to keep Mum happy and make her feel good (see? I'm not all bad!), she promised it like it was some kind of big oath that you were actually supposed to keep.

Maude has this big thing, you see, about Staying Together. It's kind of a fetish. She got it off Mum, of course – that's why we waited so long in Manchester waiting to get killed in case my dad turned up. I happen to think it's a lousy tactic. The best tactic is to stay alive – obvious or what?

She made me promise again. 'We stick together, Marti. OK? OK? I have your word, your word of honour? Promise me, Marti, won't you?' Etc, etc . . . She kept on and on, and it was obviously really important to her, so I did it, I gave her my word of honour. The poor girl had obviously failed to notice that I don't actually have any of that particular commodity. It kept her happy. I said the words, but all the time I was thinking to myself, if it came down to it, like, me or him, well, I'd do my best to make sure he went to a good place of course. Because, you know, he deserves a good home, right? And me? Well. I deserve the money.

Funnily enough, although Maude failed to do any significant 'negotiations' on that stop off, one of the guys, not the one who wanted to sell Rowan, some other guy, was desperate to sleep with her and she wasn't having it. This guy was really mooning all over the place for her. I learned later on that she'd had a thing with him before in Manc and she had a policy of not returning to her own mess, as she put it. But this guy was making his pitch worse than it already was because he was trying to stop both of us – sorry, all three of us – going further south at all.

'It's too dangerous,' he kept saying. I thought he was just trying to get her to hang around for his own nefarious purposes, but then the others started on about it too. The Bloods had been funding various different groups ahead of them to soften the place up, and the road to Nottingham and beyond was bad.

'We're getting all sorts of reports. It's really bad country down there, there's some really vicious groups going about,' said this small blonde girl, who was also trying to stop us going. Which was annoying. Because I'd made up my mind to go, you see?

For my dad? On the other hand it was making my teeth chatter with fear. Literally. I was shaking.

'I can't do it,' I told Maude. 'Look at me. You know what a chicken I am.'

'Being brave isn't about feeling no fear. It's doing things in spite of it,' she said. Which made me even more annoyed. She's always coming out with wretched pithy sayings like that. I did my best to convince her to go on her own – I even offered to take Rowan with me.

I mean, come on! That was a reasonable deal, wasn't it? It was probably even sensible.

She thought about it a bit then said, 'Sorry. The answer's no.'

'How come?' I was astonished. It was a good deal!

'Because I don't trust you,' she said. 'I think you'd sell him off to the highest bidder as soon as you saw my arse disappearing over the horizon.'

I was incensed. It was true, of course, but I was still incensed – mainly because everyone was seeing through me so easily. It was kinda making being selfish a bit redundant, you know what I mean?

Anyway, so that was that. I had a bad feeling about it. I had no idea whether my bad feels were just me being the usual chicken or some kind of foresight. In this case, it turned out to be both.

14

And it started so well when we finally set off again! *So* well. The FNA guys welded our tank up, so we were back on the road. I was being nice to Maude so I had on my combats – the proper ones, as she called them. It was a good day for biking, a few clouds but no rain. Plenty of sunshine. We'd been shown a really pretty, remote route. We were avoiding towns and villages. There was the odd drone flying overhead, keeping an eye on things – including us, no doubt. There was no way of telling whose they were. We had to park up a few times and hide under trees and stuff like that. It was a good day to stay out of sight. It's always a good day to stay out of sight.

We were enjoying ourselves. We should have known better.

We were going slow because Rowan had started fidgeting. That was a blessing, had we but known, because suddenly Maude nutted me in the nose with the back of her head, and back we all went, all three of us – stripped off the bike, head over heels, down on the tarmac – *smack bang*!

Out cold.

I got the worst of it, with Maude on top of me, although to be fair she got the washing line they'd strung across the road

104

right on her tits at twenty miles an hour. If we'd been going much faster she'd have ended up with four. I woke up a little later – no idea how long later but it can't have been that long. Maude was on her feet with her hands behind her back. Rowan looked OK except he was being held by his clothes from behind. He'd gone all quiet, all big round eyes and his face went white. The guys who'd got us were high-fiving each other, except for this bloke with a lot of muscles and a big belly, who was looking down at me and frowning. I couldn't make out much because my eyes were watering so much. My nose had been squished all over my face. Just my luck! My nose used to be quite long, but considering the rest of me it was still one of my few good features. Now it was short but it was all over my face.

What I could see, though, was that the fat one had a shotgun pointed down at my face.

'Bang,' he said. Maude screamed at him. Then he put it up and laughed.

'Just joking,' he said, in some scummy southern counties accent. Then he held out a hand to get me to my feet. Which I took – there was no way I was getting up on my own. But I still couldn't stand and I was having to grab hold of him to stop myself falling down, and he was going, 'Get off me, get off me, get off me!' and swatting out at me. But I really couldn't stand up, I was all over the place, so I was still snatching at him and getting nose blood all over him. That was the first sign that these guys were a bunch of amateurs. So he called to one of his minions to hold me up instead, and this guy who came to do the job, you know what? He was Black. Which was a surprise, to say the least, because the rest of them were white and dressed in what looked like some sort of homemade Blood uniforms, with the double cross on their fronts.

The Black guy put his arm round me to hold me upright, kind of at arm's length, like I was some kind of pollutant.

'Do I really have to do this?' he asked the big guy, who was obviously the boss.

'You have to do everything I tell you, how many times do I have to say it?' the boss guy snapped.

'Yes, sir! But, sir – this one's *Black.*'

Now listen. I have a lot of issues. You may have noticed. But one thing I don't have any issues with is being Black. I like being Black. I'm happy with it. I like Black music and Black food, I like wearing Black clothes and hanging out with Black people. Being Black is cool. If I had God come up to me and offer to make me white, I'd spit in his eyes for being the racist old bigot he obviously is. So, chicken though I am, when this Black man – he was darker than me, too, let me say that – when he said that, like I smelled or something, I slapped out at him, and he let me go, so I started to fall, so then he had to grab me again. And there I was in yet another ludicrous situation, me slapping out at the man who was trying to hold me, and him trying to only touch me with his fingertips or something, then letting me go and then having to catch me again because the big guy, and all the other guys as well, were all calling out, 'Don't you drop her, don't you drop her, Sebastian, or you're in trouble!'

The big guy, Major Tom, they were calling him, was furious. 'What is wrong with you, Sebastian?'

'But, sir, you know how they smell . . .'

'I know how they smell because I have to smell you every day, Sebastian. Damn it, you moron, you're blacker than her.'

Sebastian drew himself up – he wasn't that big, but what he had, he drew that up. 'Sir! I have to object. I'm as white as any of you. I am a proud Caucasian, sir – and you know it.'

All the guys, all the racists, they were clutching at their foreheads and wiping their faces with their hands in despair. It was bizarre! I swear to you, that brother actually thought he was white.

'That's one defective negro,' one of them said.

I was incensed, I could see Maude making movements at me to shut up, but I just couldn't help myself.

'What is wrong with you?' I yelled at him. 'Are you blind or mad or something? There's only one thing makes you Black and that's the colour of your skin, and you're blacker than I am. Pull your head up and think straight, why don't you?'

'That's not true,' he hissed. He was absolutely furious. 'Black people are ugly. I'm not ugly. Black people have horrible behaviour – they're thugs, criminals. I'm not a criminal. I behave right. I'm polite and they're rude . . .'

I leaned forward and slapped him round the face for that one, the ignorant little blasphemer, and he stumbled back in shock. Then Major Tom elbowed me away and gave poor old Sebastian a whack of his own, a really hard clout on the side of his face that must have made his ears ring and knocked him flat to the ground. Then he laid into him with his foot.

'You stupid shit, you stupid, stupid little shit, you f**k f**k f**k!' He was going. He really lost it. Sebastian – I was thinking, that's no Black name, I don't believe that's any kind of Black name – he was rolling around, trying to dodge the boot, going, 'Sir, sir, no sir, please sir,' like that. And when it was over, he got up, all tearful, and went to hide behind the other guys.

'It's not right, him treating me different from the other guys,' he wept, but Major Tom bellowed 'Shut up!' at him so hard, he nearly popped his eyes out, and Sebastian put his head down and tried to hide his quivering lip. I was thinking he only got what he deserved, but for different reasons from why Major Tom gave him that kicking. But Maude had spotted it.

'ERAC,' she said.

'We paid over five grand for this idiot and he has a new personality every fucking day!' one of them hissed, and he lashed out at poor Sebastian, who ducked to the ground and cringed there, arms over his head, for all the world like a kicked dog.

Maude was right. He'd been through the ERAC. They'd done him good. Rewritten him. I'd heard they were monetising the procedure. The poor guy had been sold as a slave to this bunch of losers, but the work was faulty. He'd been through the, 'I'm a worthless Black slave bit,' but now his own true underlying self worth was coming back. He still thought Black people were worthless, but he knew *he* wasn't worthless. So the only conclusion was . . . he was white!

Incredible.

And man! Those guys were so angry, it was unreal.

'If you say you're a white man one more time, I'm gonna shoot you in the balls,' the big guy hissed, waving his shotgun at him, so all the other guys ducked and ran out the way. Poor Sebastian looked crushed. What was going on in that man's poor head, God only knows. But he made me think about my dad, and I thought, It shows Tariq is right. The rewriting software is crap. Which means, maybe . . . maybe . . .

'What we going to do with 'em, Major Tom?' the one holding Maude asked. He gave Maude a little shake as he said it and eyed her up like a hungry man looking at a bucket of fried chicken.

'Well, we all know what we're doing with *her*,' said Major Tom, and they all laughed. 'Congratulations, Miss. This is the happiest day of your life. Times five.'

Five was how many of them there were, did I mention that? Not counting the Black man.

Maude had gone as grey as a plate of porridge. I don't blame her. None of these guys looked anything like the happiest day of your life.

I felt something trickle down my neck. I put my hand there: blood, where my nose was bust. 'Damn it,' I said, ill-advisedly.

Major Tom turned to look at me. 'And what the f**k is this?' he said.

I got a decent look at him this time, I'd been too concussed before that. Big man with a belly on him, bright blue eyes, narrowed. Very cold-looking, had his teeth bared – he'd been made that angry by poor Sebastian. He was wearing a kind of square cap with a peak, a military-style thing, and a uniform that looked a bit like the Bloods', but not quite. Big military boots, combats. He had *WA* on his hat and on a badge on his breast pocket.

'White Army,' he said, pointing to it.

I looked over at Sebastian – I hate to call him that, it obviously wasn't his real name. He looked back at me, jaw slightly down, eyes half closed.

'Sebastian, is that your real name?' I said quietly. 'Hey, man – tell me, what was your favourite food your mother used to cook for you?'

I know you must be wondering why I said that. Well, it was something my dad told me once, about how the deeper a memory is, the harder it is to write over it, and more likely it is to surface.

'Things from childhood,' he'd said. 'Early things that happened often. And smells. For some reason, the memory of smells goes really deep.'

It was just a chance, I was trying it on, really. Maybe he knew what I was trying to do because Major Tom stepped forward and slapped me round the face – a really hard slap, like the one he'd given Sebastian. I went down again. Maybe the guys at the ERAC had told him something about that, too.

'Enough of that,' he said. 'I'll do the questions and the one I'm asking you, sunshine, is, what the f**k are you?'

There was a noise behind him. The others had got fed up waiting for him and they were getting on with marrying off Maude. One of them was standing in front of her with a bible, another one by her side. The other one came and whacked her on the back of her knees so her legs gave way and she fell down on her knees on the road.

'That's how I like my brides,' he said, and they all laughed.

'She marries me first,' bellowed Major Tom.

The groom-to-be rolled his eyes and flapped his hands.

'Commander's rights,' added Major Tom. 'But first I want to work out what we have here.' He gestured at me with the gun: *Get up.*

I got up.

'Tops off for the boys,' he said.

I was so shocked, I stared at him.

'Tops off,' he repeated, waving his gun at both me and Maude in case there was any mistake. So Maude did, so I did, too. It was the first time I'd actually had 'em out on show. I was quite proud of them in some ways, although obviously they didn't match up to Maude's, which were genuinely magnificent. Still, they were a lot better than what I had a year or two ago, which was none at all. I peeled off the T-shirt and gave 'em a little jiggle. Don't ask me why. I guess I wasn't all that used to them and didn't quite know what to do. Jiggling seemed as good as anything else. Sometimes you have to try and look as if you're not shitting yourself to death, which is what I was actually doing at that very moment.

The lads all made retching sounds.

'Pants down, ladies. If that's what you really are.'

I closed my eyes, but only for a moment. I could feel, rather than see, Maude looking at me. The 'groom' dragged her to her feet and nodded at her combat bottoms, which she started to unbuckle slowly.

'I'm on my period,' I said.

'Don't worry, there's no sharks around. Pants down,' said the boss.

Now *that* I really didn't want to do. I knew what they were looking for, and if my pants came down, they were going to find it.

'I'll just need to . . .' I said. I turned to pick up my handbag. They didn't move. I don't know what they thought I was doing, but it was obviously something pathetic, because someone as stupid and ridiculous-looking as me wasn't going to pose any kind of threat. But how wrong they were! Because what I was really going for was my gun! Yes. I had a gun. Didn't know about that, did ya?

'Die, motherfuckers, die!' I screamed, because all I had to go on in this kind of situation was the movies. And I pulled the trigger. Click, click, *BANG*! it went, which was about right, because I only had three bullets. Major Tom went down, *smack*, onto the Tarmac like a sack of s**t because that's what he was, and which was utterly astonishing because I hadn't done a lot of aiming. In fact, I was looking the other way in case the gun burnt my eyebrows off. It wasn't exactly brand new.

'ARRGHGHGHGH!' I screamed and I went running at the others, waving it in the air. And you know what? They all turned and ran away.

'Chickenshits!' I bawled after them.

They ran away! Would you believe it? They ran like rabbits. Major Tom was clutching his groin, screaming, 'Help me, help me, oh no, oh no, oh, help me!'

Maude ran over to him and kicked something away – I didn't see what it was – and grabbed his shotgun.

'Now you know what it's like to have a period!' I screamed at him because he had blood all over his trousers, and I started laughing hysterically. It wasn't funny, but I was off my head. I was waving the gun all over the place until Maude came running over, picked up Rowan, who'd been knocked over in the rush to escape, and ran like an antelope. You never saw anyone run so fast. I grabbed my bag and my top and I was after her. Off we ran, fast as we could, tits flapping in the wind like jellies on springs. We ran and ran and ran until Maude was out of breath. Then I took a turn with Rowan and we ran some more until *I* had no breath left, and when we'd done that a couple of times we collapsed into a hedge, gasping.

There was a long time while we kept holding our breaths to see if we could hear anything, then panting again, and slipping our tops back on. Maude was crying silently. I was thinking how she did that quite a lot for a soldier, but then I thought – maybe soldiers do it a lot anyway but they never say. Rowan had gone into his frozen thing that he'd started doing when scary stuff happens, which was great, except you knew that once he found his voice, he was going to bellow.

After a bit his eyes moved. He looked at me and he said, 'Cry now?'

'No, not yet,' I told him. He nodded and closed his eyes. Clever little guy.

'You shot his dick off,' said Maude suddenly.

I was like, What? I couldn't believe she said that.

'I did not!'

'For God's sake.'

'I never did.'

'You shot his dick off.'

'Did I?'

Then I had this sudden image of her running to that guy and kicking something away. Was that his *penis*? And what was she doing – kicking it out of reach like it was a *gun* or something? Like he could use it even when it wasn't attached? I actually opened my mouth to ask her, but then I didn't, because . . . well, because I was too shy.

'I can't believe you shot his dick off!'

'I didn't mean to! It was an accident.'

'How can you accidentally shoot someone's dick off?'

'Maude – he was going to rape us!'

'You have to be kidding.'

'What's that supposed to mean? You think I'm too ugly to rape? Is that what you're getting at?'

'You're an idiot.'

'What difference does it make where I shot him? I stopped us getting raped and all you can do is moan. Show some gratitude, why can't you?'

'Jesus,' she said. 'Why couldn't you shoot him in the arm or the leg, or just kill him?'

'I didn't mean to! I wasn't even aiming. Anyway, what difference would it make?'

'What difference? Because now, he'll track us down to the ends of hell. You shot his *dick* off. He'll never forgive us. Ever. That was a really evil gang, Martina. They will never rest till they've got us.'

'Don't be daft,' I said. But my skin was crawling. 'Anyway, whatever they do, it couldn't possibly be worse than being raped by that bunch, they were the ugliest-looking evil gang I've ever seen,' I said, trying to lighten the mood.

'Oh, right,' said Maude, sweet as you like. 'Let me have a think about all the things worse than rape that a gang of evil white supremacist thugs would like to do to a black weirdo trans kid who's just shot the boss's dick off? Let me see . . .'

I didn't care to get involved in that conversation. We needed to move on.

So we got away, but even so it was a complete disaster. We didn't dare go back, so we'd lost the bike. Rowan's meds were in the panniers, his antibiotics and his painkillers. More importantly, so were my meds. I swear I could almost *feel* the hormones beginning their nasty work right there while I lay trying to get to sleep that night – the hair sprouting like weeds, and my temper as well. Missing the meds was going to make me AND Rowan even more bad-tempered and horrible than we were normally, so you can look out for that if you like.

And Maude's phone was on the bike as well as our food and our changes of clothes, toothbrushes, toothpaste, my flannel and wet wipes – I never go anywhere without my wet wipes. All my drugs, my uppers and downers. Back in Manchester – it already seemed like a million years away in another life, although we'd only been away less than a fortnight – my favourite shop was always the chemist. If a row of shops got bombed, everyone else would be crawling over the One Stop or the Co-op but I'd be all over the chemist. Painkillers, sleeping pills, uppers, downers, hormones, antibiotics. These are a few of my favourite things.

All gone. I could have wept. In fact, I did. All we had was what was in my handbag – make-up, gun, phone, money. You see? Maude had been giving me a hard time for taking a handbag, let alone buying a new one in Buxton. But I had some stuff at least, and she had nothing. QED.

15

Off we went, across the fields. It was hard work. Rowan had gone all limp, didn't say a word, which was great, but he wasn't moving either. We shook him and tickled him – he was normally a very ticklish kind of kid, but there was nothing.

'Trauma,' said Maude.

We had to carry him in the end, took it in turns. He weighed a tonne. He was growing so fast. It was really putting me off any lingering residual desire I might have to start a family.

We walked miles that day, creeping through the fields and hedges like wild animals, didn't dare go near the roads. I reckon the little toad was having us on some of the time at least, because he stayed like that until it got dark and we'd settled down in the remains of a ruined building in the middle of a field, when he got up and started walking and talking as if nothing had happened. No wails or screams this time.

'Dinnertime,' he said solemnly. He wasn't wrong, except there wasn't any. We'd been expecting to be in Nottingham in a few hours. Now we were still miles away, days away probably, on foot, in no-man's land with nothing to eat.

Poor little kid, he started to cry then, a sort of low level, miserable grizzle. Even I couldn't help feeling sorry for him, because it *was* miserable, sitting out on a cold night in a ruined building with nothing to eat. Maude went off to find something to drink, and she found it all right but she didn't have anything to carry it in so she came back to get us. It was some kind of filthy irrigation ditch! It was so filthy I refused to drink anything out of it, even though I was as dry as an old scab. We had an argument about it, about Rowan really. You know, Oh, he's running a temperature, he has to have some fluids. That sort of thing.

'There's plenty of fluids in there all right, I just wish they'd stay there,' I pointed out. But she had to have her own way and they both slopped it up like beasts of the field.

Then we went back to try and get some sleep.

That was the worst night I ever had. We found the driest corner we could and lay down there, with Rowan in between us to keep him warm. We had nothing to cover us, just our coats. Everything was cold: the air, the ground underneath us. It got so deep into your bones you forgot what warm was like. At least I had my music, my dad's music I should say, to play. My phone was still charged up from Matlock. I went to sleep to Parliament, which isn't my favourite stuff, but my dad loved it and if you turn it down low it's all right. Kinda. But I was waking up all night. At one point I woke up thinking Maude was touching me up and I thought, *Really?* But it was just Rowan putting his arms around my chest and squeezing me tight. Which is sweet, really. I think he got some sleep that night, but I certainly didn't and I doubt Maude did either.

So, I know what you're thinking. The gun. You're thinking – Oh, *we* never knew she had a gun. She never said anything

117

about a gun. How do we know it's true? She would have said, wouldn't she?

Like, you think you're important? You're not important. I mean, who do you think you are? You think I tell you everything? Well, I don't. There's loads of things about me you don't know and I don't see any reason you ever will. Why would I tell you everything? You think because you're reading my book you have a right to know stuff I don't want to say? Well, this is one book where it ain't gonna happen.

That old gun used to be my dad's. When things got bad he got his hands on a better one and he gave the old one to Mum and told her to put it in her bedside cabinet. She never did though. She took it out as soon as he was gone, because she didn't want to sleep next to a *weapon of death*. That's what she said, those exact words. I wanted it in my room, because I didn't mind sleeping with a weapon of death, so long as it wasn't my death, of course.

Mum never let me have it, ironically because she thought I might use it to kill myself. Yes, I have a history of depression. Once I started on the meds, the depression went away – most of it, anyway. I haven't been on antidepressants for years, but with all this stuff going on, the depression was likely to come back, which scared me almost as much as the thought of getting caught by Major Tom. Anyway, she hid the gun behind the loose brick in the old fireplace in the spare bedroom, where I found it some weeks later and tucked it away in my backpack.

I honestly never thought I'd use it to shoot anyone. When I said I only had three bullets? That was one for each of us. If things got bad. You know? If you're working for one group and another group catches you, you can expect some very bad things to happen. So, three bullets.

So I'd used one to shoot off Major Tom's dick (apparently) so now I was wondering which one of us was going to go without their bullet if those bad things happened. Not me, that's for sure! So, Maude or Rowan? I suppose it was likely to be Rowan who went without because they, whoever they might be, would be likely to be nicer to a little kid than to a pair of almost grown-ups. But you never know. Sometimes they do dreadful things to little kids to get to the grown ups. Sometimes they do dreadful things to them just for fun or their own personal perversions. So what if I did have to shoot him? Perhaps the right thing to do, I thought, was to take out Rowan and then me and Maude with one bullet. If it came down to it. Heads together, you know? Something like that. I spent quite a bit of time trying to work out what the best way of killing two people with one bullet was that night. It helped take my mind off things.

I liked having the gun with me. It made me feel good. A gun can be a very empowering thing. Take those guys who'd captured us. They were losers, but because one of them had a gun, they were winners. Until we took it off them, of course. Then they became losers again.

Yeah. And Maude had hung on to their shotgun. She slung it over her shoulder. I didn't like it – you could see it a mile off and I worried that owning something as precious as a shotgun was going to make us a target. But she refused to put it down, and really, you can see her point. The gun the FNA gave her was back with the bike. Which I guess made us and the White

Army thugs about equal, because we'd both lost a gun to each other. Except for the dick, of course. We were definitely ahead in that department.

In the morning, when we got up with empty stomachs and started to walk to Nottingham, both Rowan and Maude had the runs. That irrigation ditch, you see. What a pair of idiots! So I was right! It was great, I'm never right usually. I liked it. And Maude was wrong, which never happens either. I was dying of thirst but at least I wasn't ejecting my entire body contents out of my anus every fifteen minutes. It paid off – we found some water coming out of an underground pipe, and I drank out of that. I don't know where it came from, but at least there was nothing living in it.

Rowan got really ill. It was scary. We had to carry him almost all the way and he spent it just whimpering like a puppy. I thought it was sweet to start with. But gradually it got on my nerves and by the end of it, I just wanted to chuck him in a ditch. Poor little mite. Then his poorly finger went bad. Even I felt sorry for him, except when it was my turn to carry him, of course.

We were out there on foot for two days, the most miserable two days of my or anyone's life. I was feeling really weird just because of coming off the meds, plus being hungry. But then our luck changed when we finally walked into some coverage and we were able to call up the FNA. And guess what? They came to give us a lift! Would you believe it? Three idiot kids on a stupid mission and they came to get us. It seemed impossible until the lift turned up and guess who was in it? Tariq! He was on his way to join us after all. How's that for a stroke of luck? I was never so happy to see anyone in my life.

It turned out he'd got news of his family at last – they'd been sent to the ERAC sometime last month, so he was on his way down there too. They'd never have picked us up if it wasn't for him. Connections, see. So we finished the journey in style, bumping and banging in the back of a Land Rover.

We told them about those guys, the WA. They'd never heard of them, but they sent some people out to look for them. They never found them, though, which was a shame in so many ways.

16

Nottingham was still under FNA control, but things were moving fast and they were expecting an attack soon. The whole place was buzzing: barricades going up, roadblocks, trucks with fighters and military hardware driving about from one place to the other. And refugees. Everywhere you went, there were refugees these days. Not just Blacks and Asians. People had heard the stories of what life was like under the Bloods, the rules you had to follow, the executions and so on. If you weren't joining up, you were running away. It was like that everywhere.

Tariq and the other guys in the Land Rover who drove us were full of it – pointing out sniper posts on the rooftops, talking about mines and artillery and tactics. It looked impressive, all the effort they were putting into defending the place, but the Bloods were funded by the USA and the FNA just didn't have the right kind of weapons. You can't fight tanks, planes and helicopter gunships with popguns. All the heavy stuff had gone south for the civil war a few years ago and very little of it ever came back. Nottingham was going down, everyone knew it, but they were fighting anyway. People are *so* stupid. As if losing was somehow better than just turning round and getting the hell out of there.

'We're hoping the EU will come in and bail us out,' the guy

told us, and I thought, Yeah, you and everyone else. I remember when the first EU fighter jets appeared in the skies over Manc, everyone was cheering and yelling, like the police had turned up to arrest the bad guys. But all it meant was more bombs. They were supposed to be taking out the far right groups, but plenty of civilians got flattened anyway. There were news items from time to time about EU troops, but what can I say? I never saw any.

So the EU – all gas as usual. The Bloods, though, they were coming, they were on their way right now. In fact, in some ways, they were already there. They always had been there. Before the war you'd never have known how many people were sitting at home hoping and praying for the Muslims to be pushed into the sea, all the Black people turned into slaves – but they poured out of the swamp quick enough once they thought they had a little fire power behind them. As we drove through the 'burbs, the graffiti was up on the walls to welcome the Bloods.

PREPARE FOR JUDGMENT DAY, one said.

WELCOME HOME JESUS, was another one.

And, *THE SECOND COMING IS NIE*.

'Can't even bloody spell,' said Tariq.

'What's that about the second coming, then?' asked Maude.

Tariq rolled his eyes. 'Virgin birth, mark two. They already found the new Mary. No crucifixion this time, though. This time it's Judgment Day.'

'Does that mean we get two Christmases from now on?' I asked. No one laughed.

'We actually think we know who the new Mary is,' added Tariq. 'Some poor girl in Birmingham they kidnapped. I wonder what revolting Blood chief is going to have the honour of taking God's place.'

Yes, the Bloods were on their way, armed with the power of the new Jesus, baptising people in blood before they killed them. And Lo! It was a passport straight to Heaven, for if you were baptised in the ways of the Lord by one of the blessed, you went straight up to the angels, even if the blessed had to tear out every one of your fingernails to get you there. The Lord be praised! Hallelujah!

Nottingham was good. Tariq really looked after us. I mean, compared to Buxton it was a bit of a tip – there'd been some bombing and it was escalating, but the electrics were still on in the house, you could have a hot bath, there was shopping. I managed to get out and refresh my make-up bag, get some new clothes for me and Rowan and Maude, a new phone for Maude. The one thing I couldn't find was the thing I wanted the most: meds. I could feel those hormones swimming up to the surface. God's sake! I'd be Arnold bloody Schwarzenegger by the end of the week at this rate. And the hair! If it's not controlled, I turn into some kind of badger in moments. I went out and got myself some new razors and had a hot shower and a *total* body shave. Top to toe. No, not my head or my eyebrows, you idiot, but every other nook and cranny was as smooth as silk by the time I'd done. It felt gorgeous – for a day, anyway. After that I was in itch central. It felt like my anus had been crucified with the proverbial crown of thorns.

The internet was in really good nick, that was the best thing.

I downloaded some games and some new songs, locked myself in my room, played my games and my music. It was a Beyoncé day. I didn't let Rowan anywhere near me for the first day; he was still moaning away about his finger and pooing through the eye of a needle to be exactly entertaining. Besides, a girl needs her space – then after that me and him spent a few hours playing on a borrowed laptop. Shoot 'em ups. I've always loved shoot 'em ups – they make you feel so empowered. I'd never do anything like it in real life, but online you can be who you like. Rowan couldn't get the hang of it at all, so I had to put it away and play some miserable kid's thing, finding honey for the bears or something. He was pretty good for a three-year-old kid. I think he must have found it empowering too. I let him win most of the time in return for letting me have some time on my own. Well, it couldn't have got any less boring if I'd won, so why not?

Then, 'Marti time, Rowan.' And he'd kick up a fuss, but he let me have it.

We were there for three days and I spent nearly all of it in my room. That's where I'm at my happiest. Outside, everything was frantic. Inside, it was just me, my games, my music and the odd dollop of Rowan.

Maude made me come out from time to time just to be polite. Poor Tariq was in a real mess because of his wife and kids.

'They only took them because I'm an active communist,' he said. 'You know how the Christians hate us. They'll have been sent to the ERAC as soon as they found out they were related to me. It's all about me.'

It's all about me. He actually said that.

'But your wife is an activist as well, isn't she?' said Maude.

Exactly. 'You're being macho and self-centred,' I told him. 'And sexist. It's not all about you, you know.'

Poor Tariq blushed.

'Sorry,' I muttered.

'Don't be,' he said.

The funny things is, just a week or so ago I'd never have spoken to anyone like that. I'd have thought it, but I'd never have said anything. Things were changing. My life was changing, I suppose. That's the way it is. Life changes, you change with it. You have no choice.

Three days. Three lovely days. I could tell it to you in real detail, but why would you be interested in someone doing the ordinary kinds of things, things that you probably do every day, that you think are boring probably. Hot baths and showers. Proper food. Egg and chips! We had egg and chips. That sort of thing. I got myself in the kitchen and made a pasta bake like my mum used to, macaroni cheese, with strong cheddar and parmesan on the top. I charged my phone and ironed my clothes. I'd lost so much weight, most of them were hanging off me like a flag on a beanpole. I know! Boring boring boring for people like you, posh people who have everything they want and think they know it all. Which they don't.

Then we finally set off on the next leg of our journey. The guys in Nottingham had contacts with the resistance down there, so praise the Lord! We didn't have to actually go all the way into Blood territory. We were to meet this Bobby Rose guy at Ely, which was kind of the borderlands. Which suited me fine. All I wanted to do was drop off the software and then . . . well. That depended, didn't it? I wanted to get news of my dad, that was the thing. Ideal scenario, we could actually pick him up and take him away with us.

Imagine! Imagine that! Me and my dad together again. That would be a dream come true. Not that I supposed it would be as easy as that. They'd have to implement the software, which might not work anyway, and who knows how long that would take? It was probably just me dreaming away as usual. I knew I shouldn't do that – dream, I mean. I've learned from bitter experience that dreams like that are just the prelude to more disappointment. When did even one single one of my dreams ever come true? Never, that's when. I couldn't help it though, because even though he always let me down and disappeared on me whenever I needed him, and even though I always felt that he would have preferred a son – that's just how it was between my dad and me.

We needed to hurry, though. No one knew exactly when the Bloods were going to launch their next big push forward, but when it came it was going to make travel impossible. A lot of the refugees turning up were coming from down that way.

But we had yet another turn of luck! There was some kind of arms deal going on with the Nottingham lot and the resistance around Ely. They wanted ammunition. Well, everyone wanted ammo, and of course the FNA were very reluctant to part with any, especially with the Bloods on the move. And yet they were doing it. Nottingham was sending down a couple of truckloads of shells and bullets and Ely was sending back . . . something. What exactly, no one was saying. Even Tariq had no idea. But hey, who cares? The point was, we had a lift.

So. Bonus points for Marti and Maude for being a pair of dead lucky bitches. We got ourselves all ready . . . and then we had this stupid argument. As usual, it was an argument about me. Worse, it was an argument about *clothes*. You remember this stuff – combats versus dress, dress versus combats. She wanted me to go as a boy. Well, I had been doing that, on and off. And the thing is, I didn't like it one little bit.

All my life I had to fight to be myself. There was always a lot of pressure for me to be something I'm not, and now, what with the war and the Blood of Jesus and so on, there was even more pressure. And even though I am a complete piece of chickenshit, the most cowardly yellow-bellied person you're ever likely to meet – even so, on this particular thing I was digging my heels in. I mean, what difference would it make? I was a mixed race kid with tits going down among the most heavily armed transphobic racists this side of the Atlantic. In my own self, I'm just about everything they hate rolled up into one person. What difference was it going to make what clothes I wore?

While I was in Nottingham, I'd bought myself this really nice dress. Long narrow blue thing, bit of patchwork, bit of lace, couple of slashes around the midriff, swinging above my ankles, slit up one side, deep V down the front. Well, I put it on for the trip to Ely, and both of them were going bonkers at me for wearing it.

'What's wrong with trousers?' demanded Maude. 'Everyone wears trousers.'

'No, why should I? I want to wear my new dress. It's not even any of your business,' I said.

'Marti! As soon as they see you they'll fling all four of us into prison.'

'What is your problem, Maude? As soon as they see me they'll fling all four of us into prison anyway. As soon as they see *Tariq* they'll fling us all into prison anyway. As soon as they find us hiding in a truck loaded with ammo. What difference is a dress going to make?'

'But a *dress!*' said Tariq.

'It's just clothes, Marti,' said Maude.

'It might just be clothes to you, but to me it's *identity*. If I'm going to die because of this stupid mission, I'm going to die as me, not some dream Marti you keep trying to force me to be.'

'God's sake!' hissed Maude.

'Twowsers, Marti, twowsers,' said Rowan.

But I was like, Why are you all *suppressing* me? Why can't I wear what I want? It didn't make any difference what I was wearing, that was my point.

'I was wearing ordinary combats when we ran into the Very Evil Gang, and that didn't help much, did it?' I pointed out. 'And anyway' – I only said this to wind them up – 'I haven't got any decent trousers that fit me.' Which was an utter transparent lie.

'It's not just about you, Marti. It's about all of us. You're making our situation even more dangerous than it has to be,' said Tariq.

You may think I was being stupid. I wouldn't blame you. *I* think I was being stupid, actually, I don't know why I dug my heels in so much, but it felt really important at the time. But they went on and on and on and in the end, as per usual, I gave in and wore a pair of *twowsers* instead. But when I was done, Maude was still glaring at me.

'What?' I said.

'What sort of underwear have you got on?' she demanded, the cheeky cow.

'None of your bloody business,' I snapped.

So we had the argument all over again. I have to say I felt different about it later on when we were sitting silent as the grave going through the first checkpoint on the way to Ely. But it was too late by then. No way was I going to change my pants in front of Tariq.

Next thing you know, me, Maude, Rowan and Tariq were sitting in the dark surrounded by crates full of ammo and weaponry, on the road to Ely. And I was pooing myself again. Big time.

It wasn't a fast journey. They warned us beforehand about that. The roads were stuffed with people fleeing from the south, their cars and vans loaded up with everything they could get in there, or else gearing up their local town for the onslaught. Fighters, refugees, supplies. Roadblocks, of course. There's always roadblocks.

Not that we saw any of it, surrounded by crates. All we knew was it took hours – hours and hours and hours. Crawling along. Stopping and starting, starting and stopping. Blocked road. Roadblock. Pull over for no reason we knew of and listen to voices outside and wonder if they were going to come and search for spies wearing the wrong underpants. That sort of thing. It took a *whole day*.

Plenty of time. Plenty of time to think, to reflect and to crap yourself silly with fear.

After about 200 hours, Maude whispered, 'If you had to choose, what would you pick? Being tortured to death or getting sent to Huntingdon and turned into a c**t?'

She can be very crude sometimes, Maude. But oddly enough, that was exactly what was on my mind, too.

I hissed, '*Rowan?*' because we'd decided not to talk bad stuff when he was around.

'Asleep,' whispered Maude.

'I'd do the ERAC, any day,' whispered Tariq. 'If they torture you, no matter how hard you try, they'll break you eventually and you end up betraying everything you hold dear. Everyone does, sooner or later. I couldn't bear that.'

'The ERAC for me, too,' whispered Maude. Which surprised me. She's a tough cookie, Maude.

'Why?' I said.

'Pain,' she said. 'I really hate pain. You?'

I guess they expected me to say the same thing, but actually, the truth is that the one thing I truly could not bear is being made into another person. I've fought so hard to be myself, maybe that's why. White people never liked me, Black people never liked me. Girls never liked me, boys never liked me.

Everyone wanted me to be someone else. Even my dad didn't want me to be who I am at first, although he got there in the end. My mum was better, but even she used to have a weep over her lost little boy from time to time.

So it took me a long time to become the real me, the real Marti. Even *I* didn't know who I was for a long time, but now that I knew I was going to hang on to it no matter what.

'Wow,' said Tariq, after I'd explained why. 'You're a bundle of surprises, aren't you? You'd be quite a piece of work if you weren't so selfish.'

'That's my Marti,' said Maude, in such a way that I turned to look at her, although you couldn't see a thing in the darkness. 'That's my Marti – blue silk knickers and all.'

'Yeah, yeah, yeah,' I said, getting out my earphones. And I was like, How did she even know that, anyway?

I was playing hip-hop, in honour of my dad. Not my favourite as such, but I liked it because it reminded me of him. As the music played, I sang to myself under my breath 'I'm Coming Home' by Diddy Dirty Money and Skylar Grey, over and over and over again. Because as you know, home is where the heart is. And as you also know, I loved my dad.

17

Hours and hours and hours and hours and hours. We had to sedate Rowan, poor little mite. On the other hand, he did look much prettier asleep than he did awake. So cute, like a puppy. I definitely preferred him like that.

And the further south we got, the slower we got. Slower and slower. Stop. Roadblock. Start. Slow, slower, slower; stop. Every time we stopped I got scared that enemy guards were going to search the truck and get us. Then we got *more* slow. More bored. Stop: scared. Slow: bored. Scared, bored. Bored, bored, bored, scared. Bored, bored, bored. Terrified. Hungry. That's war for you.

Eventually the truck turned off the main road and we went faster for a bit. Then we got onto a bumpy bit. None of us had any idea where we were. It felt like a country track. And . . . finally, we stopped. We all sat there in the darkness holding our breaths, listening, trying to work it out, until the doors opened and they began unloading the empty crates. Scared. We all kept quiet, but it turned out to be the FNA blokes who'd driven us. It was all OK.

We stepped out into the open air. We were surrounded by trees, which I didn't like one little bit. I don't trust the countryside. You know? I mean, I'm happy enough looking at it, but I don't

133

actually want to be in it. The only sign of civilisation was some low, old red-brick buildings with corrugated roofs. God knows what they were. Something industrial that no one had used for ages, except that the roofs were new.

'Where's the cathedral?' I said, and everyone laughed like it was a joke, but actually, I was being genuinely stupid. Someone at Nottingham had told us about the cathedral at Ely, sticking up like the finger of God out of the fields, which were flat for miles and miles around, they said.

'It's not Ely, Marti,' said Tariq.

A very serious-looking white man in some kind of black uniform came out of the building. He was giving me that look – you know that look? Maybe you don't. A look like he'd been waiting for ages, even though he was so mighty important, to meet some other really important people. And finally they had got here – and Lo! It turned out it was me.

'Ely's dangerous,' he said. 'We're expecting an attack imminently. *Imminently*,' he repeated, just in case we hadn't got the message. He nodded his head towards . . . wherever it was the attack was coming from.

'Right,' said Maude.

'So,' he went on. 'The software.'

'What's your name?' I said, glancing sideways at Tariq. I was already getting fed up with this. We'd come all this way, put our lives in danger, and the Twat in Black was treating us like some kind of personal annoyance.

'What's my *name*?' he repeated, like he could hardly believe the cheek of me asking.

'It's OK, it's Bobby,' said Tariq, giving me an I-told-you-so look. I dug in my bag and got my phone out and I held it up. He put his hand out, but now that it came to it, I didn't want to part with it. That phone – I loved that phone. It had been my constant companion ever since my dad went away. It was like, my only link to him – and my mum, for that matter.

'You're really going to try it out?' I asked.

'No,' said Bobby Rose. 'We're going to teach it to fly.' He rolled his eyes at his men gathered around, who laughed uncomfortably.

Yes. It was just like Tariq had said. Bobby Rose was a . . . you-know-what.

The man stretched out his hand even more, but I was still hesitating.

'It's OK, Marti, give it to him,' said Tariq. I thought, We'd come this far, all the way for this. So I handed it over.

'Good,' he said, and he turned away.

'So, what about my dad?' I said.

The guy sort of chuckled and shook his head – like, *Are you kidding.* He didn't bother answering, he just nodded at the truck. 'Get back in,' he said. 'They'll drive you back to Nottingham. You'll be safe there.'

'Hey, no,' I said. Because – my dad! I don't know what I was expecting. Not this. Maybe I was thinking it would be my dad here to meet us, although I knew really that wasn't going to happen. Or someone saying, Hey, you! Look what you did! OK, maybe that's naive. But *some* news. I deserved at least some news of him after coming all this way.

'But what about him? Is he still alive?' I said.

'We've come all this way,' said Maude. She was standing

holding Rowan who was still all drugged up, lolling in her arms.

The man shrugged. 'Last we heard.' He turned away again but I took a few steps to him and grabbed him by his shoulder.

'No,' I said. Because that wasn't good enough. 'Come on! What's going on? You must have more information than that.'

He stared at me, hard. I stared back, head up, like it was a breeze dealing with the likes of him.

'I don't know about your dad.'

'Ring someone up who does,' I said.

'No one gets in or out of that place,' he said, trying to stare me down. 'People in there, they don't know their own minds from one day to the next. Now, act like a good boy and fuck off home, OK?' He looked me up down, like, *You better do as I say.*

'But my dad . . .'

'Fuck you and your dad,' he said, and he showed me his back. 'Get 'em out of here,' he called over his shoulder to the men, and headed back into the red-brick building.

'Excuse me. Excuse me, sir.' That was Tariq. 'You know I'm staying, right?' The guy gave him a quick glance and a quick nod. Well, I looked at Tariq and he looked at me. 'Helping organise things,' he muttered. But I knew what that really meant. He meant, Staying to try to find his family.

'OK,' I said. 'OK. If he stays, I'm staying too. I can help, too,' I said.

There was a pause. Everyone had stopped and was looking at me. The Twat in Black paused. Didn't even turn around. 'I've had enough of you. You get the fuck in the truck, freak, or you'll have me to deal with.'

I stood there and watched him stalk away. Didn't even bother to turn round and look at me, he was too busy poking at my phone. Well. I waited for it. The taps on the phone. The pause. The turn.

'What's the code to this?'

I folded my arms and stuck my nose in the air. 'Find out about my dad and I'll tell you. *Freak.*'

He looked at me in surprise, as if anyone would dare talk to him like that! Then he came at me – striding forward at me, yelling – 'You give me that code right now!'

But I'd had enough. I don't know why. I guess being locked up in that truck for hours and hours didn't help. And being scared. I'd been scared ever since I'd left Manchester – not that Manc was much less dangerous but at least it was danger I knew. Snipers and bombs, OK, but at least you knew what to expect. And those bodies, those children burned in the church, that didn't help. And that stuff with Major Tom. And now my dad. I'd come all this way and done all this stuff, I'd come hundreds of miles out of my way just for my dad, and now he wasn't here and I wasn't even going to find out if he was alive or dead. And Tariq was allowed to stay and I was being sent back. And now my phone was being taken off me, the only thing I had left of my mum and dad – all because this self-important, overpriced piece of knitwear was so full of hate he couldn't even be civil. He'd rather actually beat me up than do that.

I suppose he thought I was going to squeak and run, but I didn't. I made my hand into a big claw. I pulled an imaginary knife from my belt with the other hand and held it up in the air like I actually had a great big knife. I let out a great cawing war cry and I went for him like some kind of crazy valkyrie straight out of Valhalla.

You should have seen his face! It was hilarious. He came skidding to a halt and his eyes swivelled for a moment, trying to work out whether he should run or stand up for himself. Then he went for his gun, but he was in such a hurry – I was almost on him – that he got in a tangle with his own boots and sort of tripped and had to stagger about getting his balance, and at the same time pulled the gun out of the holster but got it caught in his jacket.

And then I was on him. The valkyrie from hell.

Like I say, I have good upper body strength. I used to spend a lot of time sifting through the rubble in Manc, looking for stuff, or 'looting' as some people like to call it. Plus I was off the meds, that helped. Maybe carrying Rowan around so much of the time helped too. He was off balance and I knocked him down like a snowman and had him on the floor, whacked his hand so he dropped the gun, got myself on top of him and started squeezing the life's breath out of his nasty transphobic throat. I could hear yelling and shouting around me, but no one came to stop me for a moment. Until Maude walked up – not in a hurry, mind – and pulled me off him.

'Don't actually kill him then,' she said.

I was panting. I think I nearly fainted.

'He deserves it,' I said.

'I know,' she said.

'Jesus,' croaked the guy, rolling around on his back in the dirt, clutching his injured throat. 'Jesus. Oh my God. Jesus.'

I took a look around. Tariq was putting his own gun away,

so I guess he must have stopped the guys from coming to their boss's rescue.

'Let's go,' I said, and I marched back to the truck. The Twat in Black picked himself up and went back into his hut, rubbing the back of his head. His guys were smirking away, so you could guess they'd rather liked it. A twat is a twat, I guess. They started loading the truck back up with some crates from inside the building while I sat on the tailboard and did my make-up, for the want of anything better to do. Rowan woke up and started crying. I held my arms out to him, so Maude carried him to me, and he quietened down. Stuck his thumb in his mouth and looked up at me with adoring eyes while I did my mascara.

'I won't do it again,' I told him.

It didn't take long. Everyone was in a hurry all of a sudden. When they were ready for us, I handed over the code and Tariq came over to say goodbye.

'I told you he was a c**t,' he said.

'He called me a *he*,' I said.

Tariq shook his head. 'You're a bloody piece of work, Marti, aren't you?' he said. He stood there looking at me and shaking his head. Then he turned away. 'OK, let's get this truck on the road,' he yelled. I think he wanted to make sure we were off before the commander got his nerves back. Me and Maude crowded into the back with Rowan, they loaded up the final crates, those heavy, heavy crates, whatever it was that was in them. Outside, I heard Tariq bang the truck and yell goodbye.

'Goodbye,' we yelled. 'Hope you find your family.'

'. . . Fat chance,' I muttered under my breath. The truck

pulled away and we were away with it, away, away, back to Nottingham – first leg on the road to Amsterdam, city of dreams. My dreams, that is.

And Lo! There endeth the search for my dad. Just like that.
Just.
Like.
That.

18

Once we got going again, sitting there in the blind darkness, I started to think about my mum.

I know what you're thinking: you're thinking, Wow, she's *so* weird! She spends all this time going on about her dad, goes on a Great Quest to find him, fails, so she immediately starts thinking about her mum instead.

Don't ask me to explain – I don't even know what's going on in my own head. What's more, I bet you don't either. It's only in books that there's all these nice neat explanations for things. Soon as you hit real life, that's when the messy stuff starts. So I know this is pretty random, but bear with me.

What started me off was something Tariq had said while we were in the truck on the way there. 'You're always going on about the tunes your dad picked for you,' he said. 'But you know it was more your mum who put those tunes on there, don't you?'

I'd had no idea.

'Your dad used to send her texts with a song on it and she'd put it on the playlist for him, with him away so often.'

'No one said,' I said. But I believed him at once because that was typical of my mum. Dad was great when he was there, but I could well believe that my mum was working hard to make

141

sure he was with us as much as a person who *wasn't* there could be, if you see what I mean. So she was doing that all the time – and she never told me. She let me think it was him all the time.

My mum was a pretty special person before the war broke her spirit into little pieces. When I was smaller, I was much more in love with her than my dad. It was only when I got to my teens and realised that I was not just a kid but a Black kid, and I started to think how great my dad was. I wanted to get into Black things – Black music, Black food. All that. I was like, Dad, I want to eat chicken. But not that bland buttery chicken that white folks like Mum make. I want spicy chicken, because us Black folk, we like *spicy* chicken. And curry goat and stuff. When my mum served up roast chicken for dinner I was all, Oh, it's so bland, what is this stuff, can't you put some chillies in this chicken next time? But before that, I'd just loved that buttery chicken she did for us, done in the oven with roasties. She was a good cook, my mum. That was the sort of food I ate mostly, my mum's food, because she did nearly all the cooking. Dad was away. He was only back every few weeks and then he was a crap cook anyway.

And it was my mum who first accepted that I was a girl. She was the one who took me to a gay club when I was eleven, when I thought I might be gay, while my dad was still moaning away that it was all just a phase I was going through. She was the one who took me to buy my first dresses and my first bra. My dad got there in the end, but it was always her who led the way when it came to identity.

I was thinking about all that stuff, but the other thing I was thinking was about a time that showed the difference between my mum and my dad. We were in the kitchen and they were arguing, well, talking really, about what the greatest achievements of humanity were. And my dad was going on about Shakespeare and Karl Marx and Malcolm X and various other big fellas and their Works. You know? But Mum – it was summer, by the way, high summer, a very hot day, the kind you don't get all that often in Manc – and she took a peach from the bowl on the kitchen table.

It was a perfect peach. That bowl was full of perfect peaches that she'd bought a few days ago, and now they were just right – heavy, sweet, soft, so full of juice you couldn't eat it neatly and nicely because the juice got everywhere, down your front, on your chin. It was the kind of peach that just spills juice on you. One of those peaches. And she said, 'Well, it's not those big guys. It's this.'

'What – a peach?' said my dad – like, You *crazy?*

'A peach,' said my mum. 'This wasn't invented by some big old famous guy with a big brain. It was invented by loads of little guys. When the first wild peach was found, it was nothing like this. It was a small, sour little thing, so you wouldn't bother with it. But the little guys, they saw what it could be, so they grew it and tended and bred it year after year after year, generation after generation after generation, until today, every one of us can have one of these gorgeous juicy beauties in our hand. Isn't that amazing? That's the genius of people. So that's what I think is the highest achievement of humanity – the humble peach.'

That was my mum all over. She was a very loving person before she went doolally. She loved me, and she loved Rowan and she loved Mal, who you don't even know about and probably never will, because that's something I never talk about. She loved us all.

And it was just at that point – perfect timing – that Maude cut in from her place next to me in that dark, dark truck, on that dark, dark journey, and she said . . .

'Marti, I was so, so proud of you today. The way you tackled that bully – that was fantastic. You were so brave! You're always going on about how weak you are and what a chicken you are, and look, it's not true – you're as brave as a barrel full of lions.'

'Yeah, well, he took my phone,' I said.

'And the way you look after Rowan,' she said. 'You always hold him so well and you're so considerate and loving to him. Marti, I want you to know how sick I am of hearing you knock yourself like you do, calling yourself selfish and all that, because it's not true.'

'It is so true,' I said.

'No, it's not and you know it. You're a good person, so just stop acting like a bad one and start behaving like who you really are, will you? Oh – and one more thing. I love you, Marti. OK.'

That was her piece, and she shut up then and sat there quiet in the darkness as we crawled along the road, at about 0.005 mph, because everyone else was going the same place we were going – away.

That truck rumbled along the road, and we lay hidden inside, blind as a litter of baby rabbits underground, holding our breaths as we went through the roadblocks, keeping our thoughts to ourselves.

My heart was full of all sorts of things that day. About my mum, and about my silly fantasy that she wasn't really buried under the rubble, but had slipped out in the middle of the night to visit someone and that she was there looking for us in Manchester still; and I was thinking that maybe my quest to find my dad was a silly dream as well, something that could never happen, now that he'd been rewritten by the Bloods. I was thinking about how my mum always covered up for his a**e when he was away, so we felt loved by him, and how he loved me anyway, even though I'm trans and he found that so hard, and how they both did their best to make us feel loved, despite hell and the war and everything. But they were both gone now and all I had left in the world was Maude and Rowan. And then I remembered with a dreadful shock how I'd been planning to slip away and desert them and go and save myself to live a dirty life of sex and drugs in Amsterdam, when I didn't like drugs all that much anyway and I'd never even had sex once, so how did I know if I even liked that, either? But I'd been prepared to dump them both anyway, such was the horrid lowness of my soul, as if they meant nothing to me. Yes, I'd been willing to break their hearts, but what I hadn't realised was that I would have broken my own heart too, if I'd done what I'd planned to.

Because . . . I don't know. Because we were together. Because we were family. Because we only had each other, right? I mean, look at me. What am I to the world I live in? To the world, I'm nothing. I'm not Black, I'm not white, I'm not a boy, I'm not a girl, I'm not straight, I'm not gay. I'm nothing, I'm no one to them. But my family loved me and accepted me for who I really am – my mum and my dad both. And Maude did too. She loved me, she'd do anything for me. She'd paid me back a thousand times for me helping her when she was bombed out. And Rowan . . . well. Maybe, really, the truth is, I'd do anything for him too.

What if it's really all about other people after all? Not yourself, like I always thought. Not about me. About the people you love and the people who love you?

It's a funny thing, because that was about my darkest hour. My mum was dead, my dad was as good as dead. Even though I hadn't seen their bodies, I knew it was true. I turned on my phone, the one I bought in Manchester, so I could see Rowan sleeping at our feet on a couple of blankets. And . . .

'What you doing?' said Maude.

I shook my head. I thought about how she was going to leave me and Rowan so she could go and fight and die for this benighted land. Surely she'd die, and my heart broke. I bent down and I picked Rowan up in my arms – Maude was complaining that I was going to wake him up but I didn't take any notice – and I cuddled him up to my face.

'I won't ever leave you, Rowan, I promise, I promise I never will,' I said. I was leaking tears all over him. I don't know why I was so heartbroken or why I should be so overwhelmed with love in my very darkest hour. I guess it just creeps up on you, love. That's what it felt like, anyway. You don't fall, you're just quietly overwhelmed. Maybe that's what it's like just to be human, I don't know. But that's how it was for me that day, because I was so filled with love for both of them.

Maude had gone very still watching me, so I stretched out

my other arm to take her in, and there we were, our three faces pressed up close together, wet with tears.

'I love you, Maude,' I said. 'I'm never going to leave you either.'

'I love you too, baby,' she said. Little Rowan, who was still half asleep, he put his arms up around us too, bless him.

'Never go 'way, Marti,' he said, all sleepy. 'Never go 'way.'

And suddenly, suddenly, there was so much love in the back of that truck. So much love – I never felt it before. Maybe it was there all the time, I was just too stupid to see it.

'What happened to you, sweetie?' said Maude.

'I think I must've grown a heart,' I said.

'Ah, Marti, you always had one.'

'Did I?'

'Always!'

'Shit,' I said. 'So I'm in for a lifetime of pain.'

'Nah,' she said. 'You let love in.' And bless her, that was also true.

It was strange. There I was, the ugliest I've ever been. There was hair growing out of every orifice on my body, I swear. I was growing muscles in places no girl should ever have them, my boobs were changing shape and I swear my bits were actually growing. But I was full of love. I never felt worse or better in my life.

And after that we had a big row because although I'd sworn to stick together, Maude was only staying with us till Amsterdam and then she was going back to fight. So who was deserting who? I mean . . . !

Which she didn't see at all, but it made her really angry.

147

'I've always been coming back to fight for freedom,' she hissed.

'I was always going to be a runaway bitch. Now it's your turn to put yourself second.'

'*Second?* Putting my life on the line is putting myself *second?* You manipulative cow, Marti. You haven't changed at all, really . . .'

And so on.

We didn't dare shout at each other because we had no idea what was outside. I'd turned the torch off so we had to have a whisper row in the pitch black. But in the end, guess what? I won. I won for the first time ever! Maude agreed to stay with us in the Netherlands.

'But not for ever,' she said. 'We're not bloody married. Just until you get settled.'

I was so happy, I grinned all over my ugly face. 'I probably just saved your life,' I told her. And Lo! We rode on, rejoicing. And then, maybe about an hour later, there was a bloody great bang that sent the truck swerving all over the road. Then another, farther away, and somewhere in the distance, strafing.

The assault had begun. The big Blood push. Would you believe it?

19

We drove on a while, but there were more explosions. Then a bevy of helicopters went over – the big ones, the gunships, bashing the air over our heads. Then fighter jets, flying low. Christ. The big stuff.

We were sat inside our little boxroom, surrounded by crates containing God only knows what, with no idea what was going on. If a shell hit our truck, it was going to be like hell going up. At least it'd be quick.

At some point the truck, which had been on a big road by the feel of it, turned off onto something smaller – trying to get away from the assault, I suppose. Then it stopped with a jerk. We heard the door slam at the front. Footsteps outside. Voices. The back door opens and we can hear the two drivers unpacking the crates. They lift them out one by one until they get to us, sitting there, blinking in the light at them.

And a gun pointed at us. The guy holding it waved it at me. 'Out you get.'

The two of them had decided, right there and then, that they had no chance against the kind of firepower the Bloods were sending over. So they were going to defect. Obviously! And if you're going to defect to a bunch of white Christian supremacists, you better not have a weird black person sitting in the back of your lorry – i.e. me.

'You can stay, and he can stay,' they told us, gesturing at Maude and Rowan. 'But this one – whatever it is, it goes.'

Wow, was I glad we'd all just sworn total fidelity to each other, because now Maude and Rowan *had* to get out of the lorry with me. Just saying.

'What's happening to this lot, then?' asked Maude, eyeing up the crates of stuff they were supposed to be carrying back to their 'mates' in Nottingham.

'None of it's going to make any difference at all when they have *that* flying around,' said one of them, nodding after the gunships.

'You're going to give it to the Bloods,' said Maude.

'We both have families,' said the guy, as if he thought that let him off the hook. But that wasn't a clever thing of Maudie to say, because then they started fretting that we were going to survive and tell their mates what they were doing. One of them wanted to shoot us, but the other one wasn't having it.

'It isn't like any of the FNA are going to be in the next administration, right? That's why we're defecting, right?' he said.

So they didn't shoot us. They just took our mobiles off us and packed the crates back in the truck.

'Sorry,' said the nice one as they climbed back in the lorry.

Then off they went. And there we were!

There we were in the middle of a field. A battlefield, that is.

I know what you're thinking. You're thinking, like, Oh, when she started out she absolutely hated Rowan and it was all about herself and now suddenly she's all lovey dovey? And we're supposed to believe it? So what's going on? You're thinking I'm making something up or leaving something out. Well, there is a story behind it and you may be surprised to hear I've decided to tell you what it is after all. But don't think I'm telling you because I care in any way what you think about me. I don't owe you anything – in fact, if anyone owes anyone anything, you do. You owe me for writing this in the first place. So don't go getting big ideas that you're anything special, or that because I'm telling you this story it means you now know everything. You aren't, and it doesn't. And you never will.

When I said that Rowan's possibly the most spoilt child in the known world, I was telling you the exact truth. But it wasn't his fault – it was my mum's. And it's not even my mum's fault, really. It's all the fault of some unknown scum who did something to our family, something dreadful that I never even think about let alone talk about usually. I'm telling you like the barber who did King Midas' hair told the secret about his ears. He was the only man who ever saw the king with no hat, and so he learned a strange secret, that no one else knew, that he must never tell on pain of death. But that secret was burning him alive from the inside. He just had to tell someone! So he dug a hole in the earth, so he could whisper the secret down there, just to get it off his chest. That's what I'm doing and that's all you are to me: a hole in the ground.

After Rowan was born, my mum wouldn't let him out of the house. Imagine that. He was two years old before he even went onto the street outside. She wouldn't let anyone in the house, either. He didn't play with another kid until he was two. If she'd had her way, no one would have known that he even existed. That's how paranoid she was. In the end, me and Maude nagged her into it. There was this family up the road, the Murphys, who had a little girl about the same age, so we borrowed her and took her round to play with him. It cost us six tins of beans. It was cheap, actually. It was good of them. Everyone knew how bonkers Mum was.

So this kid came round and Rowan couldn't believe his eyes. The only kids he'd ever seen were on the TV from the government channels and that isn't exactly kids' shows. He was two, she was two and half. He stood there and stared and pointed.

'Doll,' he said.

'Not doll. *Girl,*' said Maude.

'For you to play with,' I said.

We gave them both a glass of juice and a biscuit – see, we really pulled out the stops for her. She'd just got her mouth into it when Rowan let out this yell of joy, ran right up to her and tried to stick his fingers in her eyes. We were like, No, stop! He was really digging in there, the little psycho. First kid he'd ever seen, he tries to de-eye them. The girl dropped her juice on the floor, shoved him backwards, screaming her face off. He wailed, she wailed louder. Mum ran to pick up Rowan. The little girl ran to her mum, who promptly marched her out the house, both Mum and her yelling at each other. Rowan kicked up a huge fuss because his new toy had been taken away.

'Doll,' he said. 'Wanna play with dolly.' Really. He thought she was a toy.

So that was one playtime that didn't end as you might have

hoped. Psycho boy! But the real psycho wasn't Rowan, poor little kid. Like I say, it was my mum.

So now – this is the beef, you lousy gossip – I have another brother. *Had* another brother. Malcolm, after Malcolm X, my dad's big hero. He was cute. Nice kid. Darker than Rowan, praise the Lord. We all doted on him. *I* doted on him. Three years older than Rowan, which would mean we lost him at age three. I would never accuse my late mother of having another baby to replace him, but . . . well, work it out for yourself.

How did we lose him? – And this is a dreadful thing, maybe even more dreadful than just losing him at all. We don't know. He disappeared. Yep – went out one day to play outside the house and we never saw him again. Now you see, that is the sort of thing that effs with your head and as you know, I don't use the f-word lightly. It effed up my head, it effed up my mum's head and it effed up my dad's head. It was round about the time that all those rumours were going around about kids being stolen off the streets and brought up by the Bloods as Christian fundamentalists or something. You know how the Bloods have this thing about 'blessed are the little children' – so blessed that they just cannot bear them to be brought up by dirty nonbelieving Black scum like us? That.

So now you know. *That's* why my mum never let Rowan out of the house until he was two years old. *That's* why she wanted us all to watch out for each other all the time. That's why Maude was so keen on us all staying together and utterly refused to sell him to another family. That's why I found Rowan so hard to bear, because no one, no one, *no one* can ever replace my little brother Malcolm. Me and Malcolm were like two flowers on the same stem. I loved him and he loved me, and if it took me a long time to get over that and start to love the replacement, well, tough. That's how it was.

And that's why Mum and Dad had huge rows about him going away. And . . . ah, what the hell. I could go on. All I can say is, you cannot imagine what losing a sweet little member of your family like that does to everyone and you don't want to know. That's war, guys! Your perfect little brother gets stolen away and you don't know if he's dead or alive, or working as a slave, or being turned into a black-and-white supremacist, or just learning to love someone else. That's how it is. Fancy going to live in a war zone? Welcome to it.

20

The first thing we did was get off the road. It was like, road = traffic = being dead. It wasn't a major road, but it was big enough and you could be pretty sure there was going to be something nasty coming along it soon enough. Maude picked Rowan up and we took off across a field full of cows. But those cows must have been Bloods as well, because as soon as they saw us legging it away from them, they came running straight at us.

'It's just heifers, they're just curious,' panted Maude – as if she knew anything about cows. As far as I was concerned, they were charging. Talk about luck. I was thinking, I'm not going to escape the Bloods in order to get stampeded to death by heifers. Off I went, soaring past Maude and Rowan like a gazelle.

'You said they were just curious,' I shouted at her as I shot past. Then I got the giggles, and I had to stop to laugh, so Maude went shooting past me and the cows were still coming . . .

It was hilarious. We both laughed like drains. Getting over the wire on the other side was a hoot. Funny the things you remember. Bloods, bombs, snipers, burned-out churches, dead mums and dads. But those cows stick in my mind like they meant something. God knows what.

We found a field without cows and sat down to decide what to do. Well, get to Hull for the ferry to Amsterdam, of course, only a lot slower than we were half an hour earlier. We had our bags – they'd let us keep those, after searching them. They'd lifted Maude's shotgun, of course, but I had my gun stuffed down my underpants and, believe me, no one wanted to go down there. I'd tried to get some more ammo in Nottingham, but the gun was so old, no one had any. So, still two bullets left. We had a couple of small bottles of water, no food, no phones, a change of clothes or two. And that was it. Thankfully, I still had my razor with me. But no water to shave in. Nightmare! I had a chin like an electric saw.

It was a sunny day. All the May blossom was out, it had that odd smell it has, not like you expect from a flower, but I liked it because it reminded me of when I was small and we had a hedge in the garden that had hawthorn in it. I thought it would be good to just get on and walk, but Maude was scared of spy drones.

'They can be up there out of sight, you can't tell. They'll be taking pics of us.'

I was like – 'Are they really going to bother taking pics of us?'

'They do it automatically. Anything that moves.'

So we had this debate about whether it was better to go by day, when we might be spotted, or night, when we wouldn't be able to see a thing around us. Maude wanted to go at night – but have you seen how dark it gets in the countryside at night? You cannot see a *thing*.

'You're being paranoid,' I told her. 'They have cities to conquer. Why would they even care about three kids?' I mean, Jesus, there must have been literally millions of people on the move up and down the country. Anyway, she saw sense in the end – she had to, actually. We couldn't have walked two steps without falling over a cowpat in that light.

So off we went. We didn't have phones so we had no compass, no maps. We'd been driven there locked up in a truck so we had no real idea where we were, except that we were lost. Maude did one of her clever FNA things, which was to navigate by the sun, but neither of us were really all that sure whether it was working or not.

It was a nightmare! We weren't even on a footpath to start with, so we had to keep crossing barbed wire fences and hedges every fifty or a hundred metres. Farmhouses kept cropping up and we had to work our way round them because we had no idea if the people inside were going to be friendly or not. There were the drones, which Maude kept wanting to hide from – you couldn't always see them, but you could hear them a lot of the time, buzzing about up on high. Helicopters and planes kept appearing out of the sky and we always dived for cover quick then, because face it, all it took was one gung ho racist pilot with a few spare bullets to try a bit of target practice on us and that would be that. Not that there was always cover. A couple of times we got caught out in the open and just had to trudge on, heads down while someone circled overhead, getting a look at us, and us wondering if they were going to come down and strafe us. We always made a point of waving at them. Maybe it worked. We never got shot at, anyway.

And food! I mean, no food. Not having any. When you think that the countryside is supposed to grow food! I mean, where is it all? I swear I never saw so much as a sandwich the whole time. Not one bite. No cabbages or apples or even turnips. Peas and beans and things – they must grow them somewhere, right? But not where we were.

And so we got hungrier and hungrier and hungrier. We tried eating grass, can you believe that? Like cows. You know that thing when you pull a grass head and it slides out of its stem and there's a sweet soft bit at the end? Well, that's how hungry we got. We'd find a good patch and pick away at it like a bunch of monkeys, but we never got anything like enough to fill us up. We got so hungry, Maude wanted us to kill a lamb to eat. There were plenty of lambs about, that's for sure. To be honest, in the right time and the right place, I'd be a veggie myself. I was for a long time, but all that fell to bits the time I found a cellar in Levenshulme with forty-three Fray Bentos tinned pies in it. Even so – lambkins! So cute.

'It'd be like eating Rowan,' I said doubtfully.

'No it wouldn't, you're not related to any of them,' said Maude.

Normally I'm such a softie when it comes to baby animals, but right then, when I saw those woolly little babies skipping about the pasture with their mums, I didn't see cute baby lambsies at all. I saw chops and leg of lamb, all hot and wet and dripping with red, nutritious blood. Maude really got into the idea, but we couldn't catch any. She was nagging me to shoot one, but I wanted to hang on to my two bullets and I wouldn't do it, even for chops.

We were on a track. We'd got so fed up going over fences and avoiding paths and tracks and stuff, we just did it. And we came to a farm. Farms mean people. People means food. You know?

It wasn't just the food though. Rowan's bottom was being really weird – again. What I mean is, he hadn't eaten anything either, but even so he was pooping all the time. That's weird, isn't it? At least three times a day he needed to go and every time he did, Maude and I went to take a look to check it out, I mean, where was it all coming from? It was like he had a secret fudge factory up there. Without going into details, there wasn't much substance to it, but still. It hadn't exactly been possible to follow Mum's strict regime of gluten-free bread and hypoallergenic quinoa over the past few weeks. It didn't seem to be killing him, though; it was just rashes and poo.

So. Farmhouse. Food, medicine cabinet. See? It felt like that farmhouse was the answer to all our prayers, and even I was wondering if it wasn't time to utilise the gun. Maude was all for it, of course, but I wasn't sure. Farmers have guns, too, don't they? To shoot rabbits and foxes and stuff, right? So how sensible was it going in there armed with an old revolver and two whole bullets?

As usual, she took no notice of me. She was busy putting her training into action.

'If we do it, we do it properly. We sit here and we watch – hours, if we have to. We take our time. We check out who goes in and out, find out how many people are in there so we don't get taken by surprise. We check out the doors and windows. See where the escape routes are. We cut the telephone lines, of course . . .'

Off she went. Oh, she had it *all* sorted out. Who knows, it might have worked too. But . . . Someone came along the track on a tractor – one of those big blue things with wheels as tall as a shed, you know? We dug into the hedge and held our breaths as it went growling along the track and turned into the farmyard. We heard the engine go off, waited a bit longer, then got back to arguing about whether or not to raid the place. And the next thing, the farmer, the same one who drove the tractor, appeared behind us. It was a woman and she had a gun. A shotgun: two barrels. That was one each for me and Maude. And she was pointing it at us.

'Hands up.'

We hands upped.

'We're just travelling,' said Maude. 'Refugees.'

'And the little one. Hands up.' She wagged the gun over at Rowan, who was staring at her with his eyes wide and his mouth hanging open.

'Are you kidding me?' I said.

'Terrorists,' she said. And with that word, I knew we were in trouble. In her eyes, we were capable of anything, and if we were capable of anything, so was she.

'Is she goin' to shoot us?' Rowan asked. 'Will it hurt?'

'She's not going to shoot us, Rowan,' Maude said.

'He's not armed,' I told her.

'He could be wearing an explosive device,' she said. She wagged her gun at him again. 'Hands up,' she said again.

'He's too young,' said Maude, and she bent down and picked him up. The woman was holding on to that gun like it was a safety valve. She was shaking slightly. She was staring at me like I was some kind of a nightmare she was having. I don't blame her. I felt like a nightmare I was having. I was wearing my face. I had started to grow a beard. The situation was not good.

'We're not going to do anything,' Maude told her. 'We're just going cross country because we want to avoid the war.'

'We're not terrorists,' I said.

She stared at us like we were talking gibberish, then shook her head. She stood to one side and waved the gun at us: *walk*. So we walked – Maude in front with Rowan in her arms, me behind and then the woman, the farmer's wife, I was calling her, which was sexist of me because if you're wearing the wellies, you're the farmer, right? And if you're holding the gun you're anything you want to be. I nodded at it as I went past.

'You need to calm down, love,' I told her.

I don't know how I got the nerve, really. Just a few weeks ago I'd have been standing there pooing my pants, unable to utter a word. Now – well, I was still pooing my pants but somewhere along the road I was now unable to keep my mouth shut. And I was dangerous, too. If I could have got that gun off her, I'd have very happily blown a hole in her chest big enough for you to put her on your head and wear her like a hat.

I was thinking about my bag. She hadn't searched us. Some of us, you know, we have guns of our own.

She marched us down to the farm, across the yard, the gun still quivering away, and up to the door of the farmhouse.

'Open.'

Maude hefted Rowan up on her hip, opened the door and we all trooped in to the kitchen. It wasn't that big, a long narrow room. There was a sofa up against one wall, a big old table in the middle with six chairs around it, and at the other end a little fitted kitchen – a sink, a fridge, a little white cooker and one of those big cooker things, an Aga. There was a rail on it with tea towels hanging up to dry. Standing in front of the Aga was a man in his dressing gown, older than her, grey, but not ancient. As we came in, he turned round to look at us, then he put his hands slowly behind him and leaned back against the bar on the Aga.

'Hello, Jenny,' he said. 'Who's this you've brought home?'

'I found them hiding.'

'Whereabouts, love?'

'In the hedge. Plotting something, Norm.'

'What are they plotting?'

'You tell me,' she said. The gun was shaking in her hand like it had the palsy. 'You tell me. They haven't said yet.'

She was twitching away like a box of itching powder. I couldn't take my eyes off that gun. If she pulled the trigger, if she started twitching just a little bit more, she'd blow all three of us to bits at that range. We stood there, holding our breaths, trying to look like good little non-terrorists. But it's very hard to look good when you think someone's on the very edge of shooting you.

'Look at the baby,' she said. 'They're not his mum, either of them. Where'd they get that baby from?'

'He's my brother,' I said.

'Wrong colour,' she said, almost before I finished.

Jesus. 'He might be the wrong colour, but he's still my brother,' I told her. 'Mixed race. See?'

'And mine,' said Maude, which was completely unnecessary. As if the murderous old dear wasn't confused enough.

The man stood up away from the Aga and very slowly walked towards her.

'Well, we can find out now,' he said. He stepped towards her and held out a hand. 'You can give me the gun now, Jenny. I'll take care of it.'

'I found 'em hiding.'

'You did. But let me deal with it now. OK, Jen? Give me the gun, please,' he said, and he held out his hand carefully.

You could see her eyes going like marbles in her head, from us to him, from him to us, not able to decide what to do.

'They were plotting something.'

'I'll find out. Now then, Jenny – give me the gun, will you? The hens need doing,' he added.

She quivered, shook, clutched the gun till her knuckles went white. I was certain she was going to finish us off. But . . .

'Take it quick, then,' she said. 'In case they charge us.'

'Go on then,' he said. 'On the count of three . . . one . . . two . . . three, now.'

She shoved the gun at him, he took it and kept it pointing at us, but gently-like, at his waist. And there was no quivering. Me and Maude almost fell to our knees with relief, I can tell you. That woman was so scared, she could have done anything.

'They need feeding by the looks of 'em,' said the woman. ' 'Specially the baby.' Then she turned and practically ran out of the door, slamming it behind her with the most almighty bang like a shotgun going off, which made us all jump about ten metres high. I tell you, I thought the gun had gone off for a moment there. We heard her running across the yard and . . . and then . . . peace.

'Ah, Jenny, love. Sorry about that,' said the old man. 'She's not so much herself. Our son joined the Blood's Army, you know. And she thinks . . .' he shrugged. 'She thinks we're targets.'

'We're just passing through,' said Maude.

'Get you to the table and sit down. Leave your bags there,' he said. I hesitated a bit – well, you know what was in my bag – but the old guy didn't look so dangerous, so I did as he asked, sat at the table, hands on top of it. He walked back to the Aga, and leaned the gun against the wall.

'We've got nothing against the Bloods,' lied Maude.

He turned to look at us. 'My Jenny's a very pious woman, and it broke her heart when Larry went to join up. But I don't blame you for thinking we're Bloods. Everyone else does, even our neighbours who we've known for years. Now then.' He nodded. 'I were just getting some breakfast. Maybe you'd be wanting some.'

Then Rowan burst into tears. 'Don' wanna shot,' he howled. And everything went back to normal.

The old man, Norm, set about making eggs and bacon – eggs and bacon! Imagine eggs and bacon! I don't suppose you can, not like those eggs and bacon anyway, when you hadn't eaten anything but grass for days and hadn't had eggs and bacon for ages anyway. I thought I'd died and gone to heaven. And toast and marmalade and stuff. It was like there was no war. And in fact, there hadn't been in that part of the country, it had just been flying about overhead. It was on its way, though. It was

164

right on their doorstep, in fact. Even while we ate, we could hear the warplanes above.

The old man leaned against the cooker, watching us eat with his gun at his feet – he didn't trust us completely, but then who can you trust these days? Didn't have any himself, so he wasn't 'just getting' breakfast like he said, he cooked it just for us. He kept apologising about his wife.

'She was never very strong with her nerves,' he said. 'And what's happening now – well.' He shook his head. 'What Larry did, didn't help.'

He never did tell us what Larry did, except he'd joined the Bloods – the Army, as some people still called it, although it didn't have much to do with the old British Army any more. Maybe he'd been killed, maybe he'd just become a monster, who knows. Enough to break his mother's heart, and his father's as well, I think.

He was a really kind, nice old man. There was an awkward moment when Maude asked if he had any diarrhoea medicine for Rowan. He looked at us with his watery blue eyes. 'Might be some Colostomel up in the bathroom,' he said, obviously not sure how to get it down to us. In the end he let Maude go up.

'Please don't try anything silly,' he said. 'I've been nice to you, haven't I?'

'I swear it,' said Maude. 'You've been really kind, we really appreciate it.' She went up and came down a moment later with the medicine and things were positively relaxed after that.

Well, he fed us up, gave Rowan some meds and that's not all he did. He found an old plastic bottle and filled it with milk, gave us a dozen eggs, a loaf of bread and some bags of dried fruit. He was such a kind old man, he really was, because he didn't have to do any of that. He told us which footpaths to use to get us on our way, gave us a couple of good thick blankets as well and some plastic sheeting to get under if it rained. He wouldn't let us have a shower, that was the only thing, which was a pity because we all stank like pigs.

'I'm sorry,' he said. 'I'd like to. But I have to think of my wife. You saw how upset she was with strangers here.'

He did give me some hot water for a shave, though, which was a huge relief. I badly needed some identity right then. And he lent me some disposable razors. Life always feels better when you have your face sprouts under control.

Then he led us out into the yard to show us on our way. The wife, the one who caught us, was there, pushing a stiff brush up and down by one of the sheds on the other side of the yard. I saw her glance quickly at us from under her fringe and then get back to it, her back to us, sweeping away, like we didn't exist.

'I'm just seeing 'em off, Jenny,' called the old man. 'Turns out it's all right after all.'

She turned to look at us and you could see her whole face was wet with tears. It was surreal, the whole thing – like some movie. Half cosy farmhouse and half rural noir, if you know what I mean.

'Goodbye, Jenny. I'm sorry everything is in such a mess. I'm sorry we've all come to this, I really am,' I called. We were about to go, we were actually turning round to go when she put the broom carefully up against the wall and came over to us, wiping her eyes and her nose on her sleeve. Rowan immediately hid behind my legs. First thing you learn, isn't it? When to be scared.

She came right up to us and stood there, scowling.

'I'm sorry,' she said. 'I'm . . . I expect Norm told you.'

'It's OK. It's the war, isn't it?' said Maude.

The woman nodded. Then she said, 'The baby.'

'Rowan,' I said. I stroked his head. He peered out from behind my legs at her.

'You shouldn't be taking him cross country with all this going on,' she said. 'It's too dangerous. Leave him here, let us look after him. I promise.'

It went tense – like, really tense in a moment.

'We can feed him,' she said. 'We have food. It's nice . . . growing up on a farm.' She nodded around her – the big house, the barns, the chickens, the cows. Yeah. I expect it *is* nice growing up on a farm. Better than anything we could—

'Better than anything you can give him,' she said.

'Our mum'd never forgive us,' said Maude. 'So we can't.'

'You might never get there. Nor might he,' she said.

'Jenny . . .' said Norm gently.

'You can come back and get him when all this is over.'

I looked at Maude. She had that face on she gets when there's nothing on earth will make her change her mind.

'He has a mother,' she said. 'She'd never forgive us. It's not up to us.'

The woman stood there a moment longer, then without a word she turned around and marched off. Then we walked away, and I never saw either of them again. I wonder what happened to them and their son, and if they're still alive today.

It's a thing, isn't it, when the world you're living in gets so, that even complete sweethearts are prepared to kill you. We were one twitch of her finger away that day, and we'd have been dog meat.

That was a good day, I guess, apart from almost getting murdered. We spent the night in a rundown old barn belonging to a neighbour of the old man, who he said had bailed out and left, 'What with the troubles and all.' The farmhouse was nearby, standing empty, and we could have got into that, but it was the sort of place anyone would want – the Bloods or the WBA, for instance, so we didn't fancy it. But the barn was fine – under cover, hay to lie on, with the blankets the farmer gave us. It was cosy. We had food to eat. Full tummies. What more could you ask?

We always slept with me on one side, Maude on the other, and Rowan snuggled up in between, but it was a warm night for May and in the barn he got too hot and went to flop a little away from us, so it was just me and Maude. I snuggled up. Even though it was warm, I snuggled up to her. I was feeling lonesome, I suppose she was too. I had her bum up against me and one hand tucked away on the top of one of her big blowsy bosoms and I thought . . . Well, I didn't think, actually. I just . . .

I'm not a lesbian. But I *was* lonesome, and I was eighteen years old and I was still a virgin, and I stood a pretty good chance of getting killed over the next few days. And, OK – I got wood. You know. So I thought . . . *weeeellll* . . . and I gave her a little nudge with it. And then another . . .

She didn't move and I thought she was asleep, but suddenly she leaned up on her elbow and said, 'Is that what I think it is?'

I said, 'No,' at once without thinking. Then I said, 'Sorry.'

'I thought you were into boys.'

'I am,' I said. 'But you know me – any port in a storm.'

She lay there a bit, propped up on her elbow, looking away from me, having a think about it.

'That's not the best chat-up line I've ever heard,' she said.

'I know, I know!' I said. I was so embarrassed! So, *so* embarrassed.

Maude sighed. 'Anyway, sorry, Marti. I'm into boys, too.'

'We could pretend,' I said, and we both laughed.

'I can't think of you like that,' she said. 'I love you, Marti. But you're, like, my *sister*.'

I said OK. She leaned back down. I felt awful! I didn't know what was worse, the embarrassment, the rejection, whatever. She turned to face me a moment later and kissed me on the cheek. 'I wish I could, but it'd be wrong. And I think your first time should be right.'

I almost said (but didn't), 'If I *get* a bloody first time.'

That was a hook I did just then. You see? Is Marti going to get a shag or not? Read on and see.

21

We walked all the next day, and the next. And the next. And the next. And the next. Amsterdam never seemed so far away. At least we were all going together, but it was so slow! Carrying Rowan half the time, avoiding villages and main roads, cutting through the fields. That food the farmer gave us soon ran out. We begged in one village, stole from the next. Braved it out and bought ourselves some new phones in one place, so I could download my tunes and my numbers and stuff. The warplanes and drones were always overhead but none of them bothered us. We got used to them, like we'd got used to snipers in Manchester.

It was plod, plod, plod. We'd found out roughly where we were more or less – on little roads somewhere between Leicester and Nottingham. From what we could gather from people we met on the road, Nottingham was still under attack and there was a lot of fighting going on in the towns and cities along the way. Best thing for us to do was to stick to the little roads, out of the way of trouble – and head north as fast as our little leggies could carry us.

So, that was us, north, north, north, until one day, we were walking along this little country road that seemed to be going up and up and up for ever. Maude was ahead, I was behind carrying Rowan, who was being really whiny that day. He had the exploding bottom again and I was dreading that he was going to fall asleep and poo all over me – he'd done that before. He was getting weak and pale and worst of all, not holding down any water. It just went straight through him.

He needed antibiotics. We were thinking we might have to risk going into a town and find someone who could treat him properly. Then Maude, who'd got ahead by quite a way, called out, 'Hey – take a look at this.'

I trudged up the hill towards her. Up there on the crest of the hill, there was a view over the land below. There was a big road, the M1 motorway. Great, long straight thing, cutting across the fields like it had been drawn with a ruler, which maybe it had in a way. We'd seen it before once or twice on the way, but avoided it so far. It had been bombed and strafed and wasn't in such good condition any more so there were never all that many vehicles on it, but this time it was different. This time it was full of people, a great river of them – refugees, like us.

'Fancy joining a convoy?' said Maude.

'Why?'

She shrugged. 'Why not?'

'Too many people and not enough food,' I said.

'I think they've got charities down there. And meds.'

She was right. Alongside the road, you could see them. A Red Cross tent. Save the Children. Various soup wagons and kitchens. People queuing.

So we set off down the hill towards them.

*

So many people! It was a city on the move, a city of refugees, all headed north. South Asians, South-East Asians. Black folk, queer folk. White folk, too. Anyone who wasn't a Christian or who was even the wrong kind of Christian was there. The Bloods were ferocious against the kind of Christian sinner who disagreed with them. It was an insult to them, and what was an insult to them was an insult to the Lord.

And women – a lot of women. Funny thing about women, we're the only group I know who are minority when we're not a minority.

The refugees were in all sorts of a state. Some of them had been on the march for weeks. There were sick people, old people, babies, toddlers, middle-aged men, poor old biddies pushing all their possessions along in a pram or a pushchair or a supermarket trolley. One woman, not so young herself, was pushing her ancient father along, his skinny old legs dangling over the sides, draped in a sheet of plastic with only his head poking through. Shitty babies, dirty people. They slept by the roadside wrapped in anoraks and bin bags and plastic sheeting and tarps, all looking out for where their next meal was coming from.

It took us two hours to get to them, but even before we were halfway there, we could smell it: unwashed people and food. Charities, see? Save the Children was there, Médecins Sans Frontières was there. The UN was there, all sorts of people were there, doing their bit of good. There were lorries turning up doling out sacks of rice, loaves of bread, tins of beans etc. Soup kitchens, doling out soup and stew and porridge and other slop. It wasn't exactly the land of plenty cos you had to queue

172

for hours to get anything and there wasn't a lot of it when you got it. But it was food and it was there.

Of course the Bloods knew all about that column of walkers – and they were letting us know about it. Warplanes and helicopters shooting past. The sound of high-flying drones buzzing about in the clouds, twenty-four-seven. Every now and then, one of the planes decided to have fun and came down low as if they were going to attack, just to see everyone scatter – not that there was anywhere to hide. They didn't open fire – not yet. Perhaps because there were so many eyes around the column of marchers – NGOs, witnesses for Amnesty, journalists from all over the world, all there, all watching. A few times they dropped leaflets. Everyone rushed about like chickens shouting, 'Gas! Gas!' Or whatever they thought it was. But it was just paper, floating down from the sky, and no one was harmed, unless they got trampled in the stampede.

The leaflets themselves were terrifying enough. Stuff like:

JUDGMENT DAY!

THE HORSEMEN ARE COMING!

APOCALYPSE NOW! REPENT LEST YE BE JUDGED!

PRAISE BE TO THE BLESSED MARA.

Mara was the poor cow Tariq had been on about, the one the Bloods kidnapped because they thought she was going to be the new Mother Mary. Yep, Jesus was coming back. I almost wished it was true.

We started freeloading as soon as we got there: curry from some Sikh guys who'd come down from Leicester to help;

Médecins Sans Frontières gave us some antibios for Rowan. We stayed there, close to the medics, in case Rowan needed help.

Amsterdam, Amsterdam, where art thou? All I knew was, it was soooo nice not to be walking. We were both exhausted, Rowan was sick. We were stuck in the middle of the longest, smelliest queue on the planet. It was our best hope yet.

We spent a couple of days sitting around the medic place. We got coverage, so I tried to ring my dad and my brothers. No luck with any of them. Called some mates. Apparently the dairy products in Ireland were still first class, but despite my change of heart, I still wasn't enthused for cheese. Had a few other chats. I was happy enough, but Maude was too restless to stay still and she kept going off on her own – going one way then the other, looking for . . . whatever, I suppose. Some kind of an idea of what to do next.

She came back about midday on the second day . . .

'I found somewhere better to stay. They have bikes,' she said.

It turned out to be a French charity – an unofficial one – called Help the English. It was a bunch of French bikers who'd scraped together a couple of lorries, loaded them up with food and driven over here to help out and have a bit of fun at the same time. I wasn't keen, I like a good curry myself, I'd rather have hung out with the Sikhs, but old Rubblehead was fixed on it. So off we went. It was only about a mile up the road, to be fair.

So these Frenchies, they'd built a brick oven by the roadside and scraped together enough wood to get it hot enough to bake bread. When we came along they were handing out warm loaves, and it smelled beyond delicious. And pots of lamb stew. They didn't have any refrigeration, so I'm guessing they got the lamb from the same place we didn't. It was great. Yeah, they did good food. In fact, it turned me on to French food. Stuff like confit duck – that's duck in a tin in its own fat, for the ignorant among you. Sounds disgusting, *non*? It's not. Well, it wasn't then, but we were starving hungry. Usually they doled you out just potatoes in the fat, which was also delicious. But sometimes you got a piece of meat, too.

They'd put up tents by the roadside and fed people as they went by.

''Ere you go, you poor *Eeenglish* peasants,' they were shouting, doling it out, '*Haute cuisine à la* M-One. 'Ow can you *reeseest*?'

They were a laugh, with their piercings and tats and leathers and big beards, although some people hated it – you could see from their faces how much they hated being poor *Eeenglish peasants* who had to take charity from a bunch of hairy French bikers. Maude had already made her mark, and as soon as we arrived she was chatting away to them in French. Especially this one guy, tall and skinny with his beard in a plait and a pair of huge rectangular sunnies, like TV screens, they were. I didn't see any bikes. I reckoned if there was going to be any kind of bike around that camp, it was likely to be Maude.

I was sooo jealous! Of Maude's French, I mean. I'd spent half my life being jealous of Maude. She'd had better schooling than me – her parents could afford tutors and all that, plus they had holidays over there, too, whereas we never went abroad. Our kind of family never does that kind of holiday. We only did days out . . . But who am I kidding? I never did any work even when there was school. Anyway, she was gabbling away with them, and I was . . . you know that thing? Where people start gabbling away in a language you can't understand and all you can do is stand there like an idiot and wait. That was me.

There were a couple of women, a couple of kids and four men, all of 'em eyeing me up curiously, which I was in no mood for. But one of them caught my eye. Medium-sized guy, with short hair and a blond beard. In his late twenties. White, but with a deep tan. I don't like 'em too pale. I turned my head to watch him watching me, and he looked away, looked down . . . but then his eyes came back up to meet mine. And he smiled.

Yeah. Yeah. He just smiled and I smiled back right away, because . . . well, I don't know why. We recognised each other, maybe. Which, if that was the case, would be the first time in my life I'd recognised someone recognising me and been fairly sure about it. I looked away too, but then I got my courage up and I looked at him again, and he looked back more or less at the same time and this time we gave each other the nod. And we laughed because . . .

Because.

Maude turned to look at me, as if I'd spoken out of turn. I shrugged. She turned to ogle the blond guy, looked back at me, like – really? Then she went back to gabbling in *Francoiseaise* to the tall skinny guy, who she clearly thought was some kind of prize catch. I was thinking, Too skinny. *My* guy had a nice layer of fat around his ribs. I don't like 'em fat but I don't like 'em thin, either – and I was just thinking it would be nice to dig my fingers in there and see how ticklish he was, when he nodded at me again and went off to get on with the cooking.

I got fed up waiting. I'd put Rowan down and the women were making a fuss of him, showing him to the other kids there, so I parked myself down by the lorry against one of the wheels, still waiting for Maude, and as soon as I sat, I was exhausted. One of the women – chubby girl, her name was Laetitia – she came over and sent me to one of their tents to lie down and sleep.

'Are you sure? Are you sure?' I kept saying.

'Yes. Yes, yes,' she kept saying, which was about the limit of her English. So I went to the tent and – pop! I was gone. Fast asleep.

And I slept and I slept and I slept. I had no idea how tired I must have been.

When I woke up it was quite late in the afternoon. I lay there for a while, listening. They were still talking away in French. You could hear the sound of the refugees as well – a babble of voices beyond like a river. The odd lorry moving around, people talking in English, Punjabi. There were Caribbean voices, posh voices, poor voices. All sorts. Mainly immigrants, or people whose parents or grandparents had been immigrants. So many different kinds of people, and all of them *wrong*. The wrong colour, the wrong voice, the wrong beliefs. All of us united, wrong together.

Then I had a sudden pang about Rowan and I got up to go and see what was going on. But it was fine. He was playing with the other kids, two French kids. They'd decided he was a baby, and they'd wrapped him up in blankets and were feeding him out of a cup with a spoon, and milk out of a baby bottle they'd got from somewhere, which made me laugh. It must have been heaven for Rowan. He was lying very still and going, 'Ga-ga,' like he thought a baby did. One of the little girls kept squeezing the bottle to make the milk come out, which I thought was hilarious. I mean! He didn't even have to suck!

It was quite a mild day, but it had been damp and I was a bit chilly. Laetitia gave me a shawl to wear. They were all very kind. They fed me, gave me a big plate of fatty potatoes with a bit of meat in it. It was just heaven. Then I was tired so I went back to sleep, but only for a short while. When I got up again, everyone was cooking. Maude was there too and I joined in, peeling spuds.

So they sort of adopted us. How cool was that? I might have known that whenever it looks like Maude's on the hunt for a shag, there's usually another agenda going on. She always was clever when it came to using her assets.

I did about half a tonne of potatoes that day. My guy, the blond guy, Anton, he was called, was one of the cooks, him and Laetitia. They were working a little way off. After a long time he seemed to finish whatever he was at and walked round to where we were and smiled at me again. My insides melted a bit. I wondered if he'd come round just in order to smile at me. Then he went off to his tent. I saw him duck down and go in, and he cast me a little glance as he went.

I did some more spuds. Then another woman, Marie, took the peeler out of my hand. 'Enough,' she said. Actually, my hands were sore, I had blisters. I wasn't used to the work.

'You go.' She waved her hand around the camp.

'Do you mind?'

'No, of course.'

'Thanks.'

So I wandered off. Marie turned and said, 'Take your time.' Laetitia, who had come to help with the spuds, leaned over and said something quietly to her, and Marie answered and they both laughed softly.

'*C'est là-bas*,' said Laetitia.

'*C'est* what?' I said.

'It's over there,' translated Marie, nodding to one side. ' 'Is tent. Over there.' She was pointing over to where Anton had gone.

I was—oh my gosh! Was I really that transparent? I fled, I just fled. So I had to wait ages for them to stop working so I could go and hang out around his tent.

I wasn't even sure he was still in the tent by then, actually. I was faffing around, looking for something to do, but there wasn't anything *to* do. I was too shy, still way too shy to do anything myself. And I wasn't sure. I mean, really – how can you ever be really sure? And I was terrified of being rejected. I was wondering if maybe I ought to go and cadge a ciggie, but I don't smoke. Or go and ask him something, but there wasn't anything I needed to know.

'Hello,' he said. He made me jump, he came out so quietly while I was looking the other way.

'*Bonjour*,' says I, trying to look cool.

We both stood there and it was just getting awkward when he said, 'Would you like to come in for a little drink, perhaps?'

His English was very good – it sounded just like that, with not much accent at all.

'I don't drink,' I said almost at once, without thinking, even though I do sometimes, and he nodded and looked awkward, so I said, 'I'll come in anyway if you like, just to be sociable.'

And he smiled and I smiled, and I went into his tent, you know? And I thought to myself, Can it be that I'm actually growing some instincts, because I swear, I never had any instincts for anything before that. I never knew what people were doing unless they told me straight out, I never knew what things meant, or how to behave or anything. But I knew what he wanted that night, and I knew I wanted it too. So I went into his tent, and Lo!

Lo. It came to pass.

I know what you're thinking. You're thinking you want to know how it happened and maybe who said what and who did what and how and to who. Well, dream on. Because listen, honey – you are nowhere near that special. Nowhere *near*.

Later, Maude poked her head in the tent.

'OK?' she said.

'OK,' I said. She was giving him the eyeball. He had a ciggie halfway to his lips.

'OK?' he said.

'She's my sister,' said Maude. And she gave him a look, a good hard look. Then she went.

'Wow,' he said.

'Sorry,' I said.

'Your sister, not your mother?' he said, because she was so obviously checking up.

'She was just making sure.'

'Why?'

Well, I knew. It was my first time, you see? My first lover. I know, I know! I'm a late developer. I didn't tell him that, though. He was lucky enough as it was, as far as I was concerned.

Later, when I was getting dressed, he was laying there watching me, and he said, 'You are very brave and you are very lucky.' Out the blue, just like that.

'Why?' I said.

'The way you dress.'

I looked down. I'd fetched my bag into his tent and put on that blue dress I told you about. Somehow it had really grown on me.

'What's wrong with it?'

'Nothing's wrong. It's very brave, that's all. Anyone else in this place, at this time, they'd go in disguise.'

'This *is* a disguise, you should see what I wear when I'm at home,' I said, which made him laugh.

'You could dress like a boy, it would be easier,' he said.

I shrugged, but it hurt. Yeah, I *could*. More than ever really, since I'd lost my meds and all the old evils were creeping up on me. My face was as hairy as a witch going through the menopause. Even though I was shaving every day. My tits were turning into moobs. But I'd tried that disguise stuff and it never did me any good that I could see.

The way I felt then, I was holding my breath until I got my

181

hands on some meds, found a decent hairdresser and got some identity back. That was the feeling.

'It wouldn't be me, then, would it?' I said. I was crouched down looking in a little mirror I keep in my handbag to sort out my hair, which was a mess. 'What do you mean about lucky, though?' I asked. 'No way on this Earth am I ever lucky.'

'Your friend lets you dress like that,' he said.

'What's it got to do with her?'

'It draws attention to her too, of course.' He frowned. 'You don't *know* that? Then you must be an idiot, Marti,' he said.

He was right about that, anyway, because I am an idiot. I was actually surprised – can you believe that? Even though she'd been on at me about it all the time, and Tariq too, even though we'd had all those rows about it, somehow I still didn't get it. All the time I just thought about how they were being inconsiderate about my identity. Funny, eh? How you can be told something over and over and still not know it.

I told you I was a selfish cow.

I went out and found Maude and I gave her a big hug and a kiss, but I didn't tell her why. But I made up my mind that while I was here, with the Frenchies, I was going to be myself for Anton, but that when we went on the road again, I'd do like Anton said and go disguised as a man. But gladly this time. It was something I could never do for myself, but I could do it for Maude and Rowan, I guess.

I spent almost the whole of the next three days in that tent with Anton and I'd have spent more if we hadn't had to move on.

Sometimes I think I could even have loved him, but I don't know. I'll always remember him, though, and not just for the sex. The sex was good, you know, but after a time the sex fades in your memory. But that little conversation I had with him never left me because I knew that he was right. I *was* brave, if I had to be. If it was for the right thing. Of course there were plenty of other things where I was still the biggest chickenshit that ever walked the Earth.

But it was good to know that about myself, and Anton – if you're out there – thank you so much for telling me so.

22

Three days, three lovely days. When I look back at that time in my life, which has had so much that's terrible in it, that little bit of time with Anton and the Frenchies was like a bubble of pleasure.

What's more, there was good news on the war front. Some serious resistance was going on in the south. There was fighting in north London, around Watford, all the way out to Hemel Hempstead, round that way. And in the east, around Huntingdon, where the ERAC was. The Twat in Black might have been a twat but that didn't seem to stop him kicking some ass. Apparently the EU and some of the Middle Eastern states had started providing some proper assistance, including warplanes, heavy artillery and so on.

So the Bloods weren't getting it all their own way for a change. You couldn't exactly say they were in retreat, but they had pulled back from the northern front. Retrenching. Nottingham was still under their control but they weren't likely to be pushing further north any time soon. Finally! We had a break.

Funny thing, I barely even thought about it at the time. It was just all part of the golden glow. All I was worried about was when I was going to get some time with Anton again. Rowan was busy playing, sleeping and eating, which is about as good as it gets for a three-year-old. Maude was with Philippe, her skinny bloke, the boss man of the outfit, which must have suited her to the ground judging by the big fat grin she had plastered across her face the whole time.

One disappointing thing: no news from the ERAC itself. Of course no one really knew much about it, it wasn't public knowledge by any means. People had other things to worry about, but I was dying to find out if that software had worked or not. If it had, then the fact that there was some proper resistance going on round there was good, and . . . my dad. I mean, I'm not an optimistic person, as you'll have gathered by now. But still . . .

I asked and asked anyone who'd come from round there, and at all the tents and so on, but no one knew a thing. Most of them hadn't even heard of it.

What can you do? Just survive and enjoy the days when you can. And I could. So I did.

So. I woke up in the middle of the night and there was Maude with a hand on the side of my face. Soon as I opened my eyes, she lifted a finger to her lips.

I got up on one elbow. Anton was fast asleep next to me. Rowan had slipped through the front of the tent and was standing behind her, his cut-off finger in his mouth. He took it out and put it to his lips like her and said '*Shush!*' in a too-loud whisper. Maude turned to glare at him, then crawled out backwards.

I got up, quiet as I could, and slipped out after her.

'What's going on?' I whispered.

'Time to go,' she said. Before I could ask why, she shook her head and motioned me to follow her. I tried to get to my rucksack, but she stopped me, so I just grabbed the handbag and a handful of clothes. No questions. Then off we went, weaving our way in between the Frenchies' tents until we got to the two lorries the guys used, parked up right in the middle of the camp. Maude whipped out a set of keys, shushed me again, and opened up the back of one . . . quietly, quickly.

'Maude? Why are you opening up their lorry? What's going on?' I whispered. But she shushed me so fiercely, I shushed. She put down the tail flap – she even made me help her, the bitch, because if they caught us fiddling with their stuff, we were dog meat. Even with Anton on my side, we were dog meat. I had no idea what we were going to find. I'd only ever seen inside the other lorry, which was the one they kept the food in.

But I guess it was predictable. Bikes. Four big, fine motorbikes. Right at the front was a dirty great shiny chopper, with the front wheel half a mile in front on its long spokes and an engine as big as the moon. It was a moonlit night, and I tell you, it looked like an angel sitting up there, shining sweetly and softly in the silver light.

I was like, WTF? I mean, Maude always loved a bike, but . . .

Then she got out her knife and started slicing tyres.

'What are you doing, Maude?' I hissed, clutching hold of her and trying to be quiet. We were surrounded by bikers! I *mean*! 'These people are our *friends*. God's sake!' I was beside myself!

But she shook me off and got on the chopper – the only one whose tyres she hadn't slashed – hoisted Rowan up behind her, and nodded for me to get up behind him.

I stood there. I was shaking, I think.

'But. But, Maudie!'

She didn't answer. She pulled down the little silk scarf she'd started wearing the past couple of days.

'*Look*,' she hissed.

So I did and . . . yeah. All around her neck. Bruises. Deep, deep, dark bruises.

'Jesus. Who did this?'

She patted the chopper. 'Phillippe.'

'This is his bike?'

'Oh, no, no, *no*. This is *our* bike.' She lifted up her top to show the bruises on her side. Rolled up her sleeves to show the bruises on her arms. Jesus. He'd really done her good. Never where you could see, though.

'You with me?' she said.

'Always,' I said, and I got on the bike.

'Ready?' she said.

'I thought you were happy,' I whispered. 'You had that big smile on your face.'

'This one?' she said, turning round and grinning at me.

I had a good look.

'That's the one,' I said. Yeah, and if I'd been paying proper attention, I'd have seen how fake it was.

There was a shout. They were up! One of 'em at least. Maude started the beast up, revved the engine, and off we went! Off the end of the lorry, right in there amongst the tents. Someone was charging us, I couldn't see who it was, but tents were opening, people were getting out. Maude drove round the guy charging us, gave him the slip.

I could see Phillippe crawling out of his tent, and Maude headed straight for him – actually, she did a curve to get to him, which was entirely unnecessary. She didn't have the speed. He dodged out of the way, but I put out my fist and whacked him one. Thing is, I didn't just get him with my own puny Marti-strength. We weren't going that fast, but even so, I had him with the speed and weight of his own chopper. Bang! He went down like a rock. I almost came off myself, and we swerved and almost stopped. His mates were up, running after us. Maude twisted the bike, hit the edge of his tent and there was a terrifying moment where it nearly got tangled in the wheels. People were waking up all over, coming out of their tents and bivvies to see. Maude was weaving and crisscrossing, but even though she was used to bikes, she was having trouble with those long forks on the chopper. There were obstacles everywhere. Rowan was yelling and screaming at everyone. Torches flashing, people yelling. I looked round behind and Phillippe was right there, and I swear he was about to pluck me off the back, he was running so fast on those long skinny legs. But then out of nowhere Laetitia appeared, and she just threw herself at him, and down he went again. That was it. We were out of there, we were free! Maude weaving as fast as she could round all the people and tents, going so fast already. I had to hang on, but I got one more glimpse of Phillippe back on his feet, holding Laetitia by the throat and roaring into her face, but there was the other woman, Marie, running up behind him with a pole, and others to help her. I like to think Anton was there, but I couldn't make it out. I saw Marie draw that stick back and she was going to whack him right at the back of his knees. Then Maude hit a pothole and swerved and I had to grab hold of her and snatch at Rowan to stay on.

She put one foot down, got her balance back . . .

'For the sisterhood!' I bawled. Maude put her head down and opened up the throttle. The road was full of people waking up fast and jumping up to see, but we flew past them. She found a clear bit in the gully by the hard shoulder where she could pick up speed, and before you knew it we were on a slip road. Up and away and off onto the country roads, roaring like a lion, flying like the wind, like the devil was behind us. Which, if his name was Phillippe, he very probably was.

And, yes, you can bet I was sad about Anton. So sad! But no one messes with my Maudie, no matter how soft their friend's brown eyes are, no matter how warm their hands, no matter how well their lips know how to kiss and where and when. Just don't you dare!

So we got two miles down the road, and the bike failed. It spluttered, it coughed . . . it died. Maude cursed, tried to restart it. But we were out of fuel. Those boys weren't that stupid. Well, they were stupid enough to leave *some* fuel in it, but not stupid enough to leave it full. Either way, we were two miles from the vengeance of Phillippe, with no fuel, on a bright moonlit night.

We wasted a bit of time faffing about with the bike, before we realised what was going on. We hadn't even set off to hide when we heard them coming: the other bikes, on their way. It hadn't taken them more than a few minutes to change the tyres and refuel and now here they were right after us. By the sounds of it they weren't far away, already off the motorway. Neither of us said a word. Maude picked up Rowan, I picked up her backpack – I didn't have one, she hadn't let me gather anything up from my tent in case Anton woke up, so all I had was my handbag. Yes, girls, you never see me separated from my handbag, even in an emergency like this – and then we ran across the fields until we found our old friend: a nice fat, prickly hedge.

We could hear them clear as anything, driving about the lanes, looking for us. They found the bike after about fifteen minutes – we'd not had time to hide it properly. There must have been some network coverage there because they converged on that spot quickly enough. Then they started walking the fields, trying to find us, which was terrifying.

Phillippe was shouting: 'I get you, you bitch! I cut your face. I pay you for this! I get you both!'

They had torches, sweeping the hedges and the fields. Rowan was doing his clam-up thing – he sort of went into a trance whenever we were in danger, which was a relief. It was poo-your-pants time again, folks.

I say *they*, but we weren't sure how many of them there were. The girls weren't there, I reckon, and I never heard a squeak out of Anton. So two or maybe three of them were on our case. If there had been six, they'd have got us most likely, but as it was, they didn't.

Eventually the bikes started off again. They roared around

up and down the lanes, being all macho, I guess, to make up for not catching us. Then they headed off.

The noise died down. Were they gone? Were they hiding and sneaking back? We were like, What if they've left someone behind to listen out for us? So we had to just sit it out. That was one looooooooooong, *looooooooooong* night.

In the morning, we were still nervous enough to hide ourselves away. But they never came back. Maybe in the end getting the bike back was enough. Maybe Phillippe wanted to hunt us down, but the others weren't so keen, even the ones who came out the first time. They obviously knew how he treated his girls.

That's my Maude – always the one with the plan. She was prepared to put up with anything she had to, if it helped us reach our goal. She knew pretty quick what Phillippe was like, but she put up with that – got the keys, waited for when he'd had a skinful to drink. Every night he liked to hurt her. But she got her own back all right. The only shame about it was that I didn't have long enough with Anton. And that the bastard got his bike back at all.

23

So there we were again – on foot, in the countryside, not sure where we were, navigating by the sun. Climbing over fences, hiding in ditches and getting cut on barbed wire. I had nothing except my phone, my handbag, make-up, a gun with two bullets in it, a lighter, my gold coins – but not even a change of clothes. And no meds and no *razor*! I was beginning to look like Benny the Bear. So much hair! I don't know where it was all coming from.

I had my long blue stretchy dress that I bought in Nottingham, and my daisy DMs. That was it. There were no shops in about a million miles – I'm not even sure they'd invented them this far out in the sticks but Maude lent me some combats and a khaki top from her extensive wardrobe of extremely dull militarist garb. It was too small but I wore it anyway, in light of what Anton had said to me. With that and the stubble, I did look less conspicuous. It's all relative, innit?

So it was plod, plod, plod, hour after hour. I don't suppose we got more than a few miles each day, especially with Rowan. At least his tummy was finally better. After the first day, the hunger kicked in and pretty soon that was slowing us down as well. Try walking on an empty stomach. You won't believe how tired you're gonna get.

It was boring. And tiring: plod, plod, plod . . . plod, plod, plod. After the first day we decided that the Frenchies weren't coming after us, so we got off the fields and started to walk on the country roads. To be honest it might have been just because we needed the going to be easier. We thought about getting back onto the M1, but the idea of Philippe tearing up and down the motorway and finding us put us off. Anyway, we both preferred the small roads. Quieter. The fewer people, the less trouble, that's how we thought about it. If the Bloods ever did go for the refugees, it was going to be the crowds they'd want, not the dribs and drabs on the little roads. It did make food harder to find, and it left us all the more at the mercy of the weather. We didn't dare let Rowan get wet too often. He was only a little thing, a scrap, always bloody ill and a few good cold drenchings . . . you know? He could actually die on us, out here in the land of no meds. Fortunately it was summer and not too cold. When it rained though, if you got caught out in the open, you had a problem on your hands. Luckily Maude still had the tarp the nice old farmer gave us.

Things were much more relaxed this time, though. With the Bloods occupied back down south, there were no warplanes overhead, not so many drones, less pressure, less danger. It was hard, but it wasn't as stressed. There were other people like us on the road, people who didn't want to be part of the main crowd: anything from lone travellers to a mum or dad and a kid or two, right up to big households on the move. We teamed up with them sometimes for a while until one or other of us decided to go another way, or camp up for a few days somewhere or whatever. We passed through little towns and villages. People were often prepared to help us out. Maybe they'd give us a meal, or some spare clothes, or some spuds or pasta or a loaf of bread. Sometimes we'd stop off in a village for a day or two to shop or beg, gather a few resources, then move on. My money was running low. I bought some new underwear in one place, and I got Rowan a toy plane, which he loved to fly as we toddled along – it kept him going for hours, that plane. His only toy. I also got Maude a necklace with green stones to suit her eyes, and she looked at me like I was being an idiot.

'Just because you're a soldier, doesn't mean you can't look good,' I told her.

'Waste of money,' she said. She wore it, though.

Some places were good, some were dreadful. Some places, the police moved you on, others they directed you to a better spot. Some places you'd wake up and there'd be a bag of food or clothes next to you, some places you got beaten up as you slept. We got peed on once – even Rowan. I ask you: who'd pee on a child?

We had one guy let us sleep in his garage for a couple of nights. We had another family invite us round for a meal. Rowan was actually an asset – like I say, he was light-skinned and cute, and even Black people like light-skinned people. So, we made our way. Yes. We made our way. I'd go so far as to say, we were getting there, the three of us. Sticking together all the way, just like Mum said.

We'd been on the road maybe ten days and we'd made good time – we steered our way around Nottingham, which had fallen by this time, and we were up on the roads east of Sheffield. We were doing OK, keeping up the good pace because Sheffield was obviously going to be next on the Bloods' list and we needed to keep ahead of them if we could. We teamed up with a white family, the Hamiltons, nice folk. They were on their way up from Leicester because they simply could not bear to live with the Bloods, even though all they'd needed to do was say, 'Yes sir, no sir,' and follow the rules. You have to respect that. Their son Steve was sniffing around a bit, and I was flirting with him – I even put on my girlie gear, which drove him crazy. We were miles from anywhere so I figured it couldn't do any harm. It was fun, but I just didn't fancy him enough. Maybe I hadn't got over Anton, I don't know. I was like, Two in just a few weeks, after not having any for eighteen years? That's, like, being a slut. Don't get me wrong, I hadn't given up on being a slut. I just figured you had to practise a bit before you got there.

We arrived at a little hamlet, right in the middle of nowhere. It was just a few barns, a big farmhouse, a smaller, more modern house and a cottage or two.

That wasn't unusual, there were plenty of farms about the place, quietly going about their business. The country might be being torn to pieces, people were dying, there was torture, mayhem and cruelty everywhere, but everyone still had to eat, earn a living and get on as best they could. What was unusual about this place was it had been shelled.

It was miles from anywhere, nothing going on. It didn't look any different from a hundred other farms we'd seen. Who'd want to bomb a farmhouse way out here? But there it was. There was a shell hole in the side of it, a couple of craters in the yard and more in the fields around. Someone had actually sent missiles to get the job done. The roofs were all fallen in and the whole place had been scorched. It must have been an inferno in there, you'd have been able to see it for miles around. Bullet marks on the walls. Whoever it was had done a very thorough job.

We wondered if it was the name on the farmhouse gate: Jerusalem Farm. Christians weren't always so popular now. Or maybe someone had been making bombs there, or . . . who knows? Either way, once it had been a place to live. Now, there was only death.

This other family, the Hamiltons, they just wanted to get out of it as fast as they could, but Maude and me were desperate to have a look. We were a bit more battle-hardened than they were. And we were hungry. There might be food hanging around in there somewhere. The trouble was that charred smell in the air. It reminded me of that other village, the one with the burned out church.

'What if they come back?' The woman – Jane, her name was – wanted to know. 'And they'll have looted it, won't they?'

'Not necessarily. Looks like a missile attack,' said Maude. Yes, we regarded ourselves as experts in this field. In the end, they decided to wait in a little conifer plantation nearby and keep an eye on Rowan for us while Maude and I went ahead to have a look.

Like I say, whoever had done this place over, they'd done a good job. It was in bits. There'd been a good number of hits. Even so, it was one of those really old places with walls about a metre thick, so although most of the roofs were down, most of the walls were still standing unless they'd taken a direct hit.

We snuck around, keeping quiet, just in case. Gradually we began to feel safer – it really felt like there was no one there. You get a feeling for that sort of thing. There was lots of stuff lying around, so it seemed perfectly possible there might be food. We located the kitchen easily enough, even though it was under a tonne of stone roof tiles. We dug around – and yes! Pay dirt. Tins! Yes, yes, yes! Tins of tuna! Tins of peas, tins of beans! And God bless – I remember thanking the Lord who I don't believe in for this – a box with pot noodles in! Under all those tiles, the fire hadn't got to them. And they were still dry. It was a miracle! Hallelujah!

And then from nearby a baby cried.

We both froze. We crouched down, because where there's a baby, there's people, right? We thought maybe it was the Hamiltons come to help, they had a baby. But this was a *different* baby. Different voice. And weaker. Perhaps very weak.

We crouched down there in the wreckage, sheltered under a slab of fallen roof. It felt suddenly very still.

'Let's get out of here,' I said.

Maude paused.

'What if it's in trouble,' she said.

'It *is* in trouble. So are we. We need to get out of here,' I said.

'Right,' she said. But neither of us moved. We waited a bit. We waited a bit more. We kept very still. The baby stopped.

'You reckon it belongs to someone?' I asked.

'Don't know.'

'You reckon it's sick? You reckon it's hurt?'

'I don't know,' she said.

We waited a bit longer. The baby began to whine. It coughed

once or twice. It cried again, just very briefly, a couple of wheezing croaks. Then it fell silent.

'Jesus Christ,' said Maude, because that baby, it broke your heart. It was a *baby*, for God's sake! It was hurt. You could *hear* that it was hurt. There was no one to look after it. It might have been dying, right there and then. You have no idea how terrible and ferocious babies are. They can break your heart at a hundred paces and there's no weapon on Earth can stop them.

We waited some more. After a bit it wailed again a few times. The sound was so thin and weak. Then it was quiet again.

I was thinking, Just our luck. Another damn baby!

Maude let out a big, long sigh. 'I better go and have a look,' she said.

'You sure?'

'No.'

'What if it's a trap?'

She paused, thought about it. 'There's no one here,' she said. 'I expect it's been left, its parents will come back. But . . .'

I nodded. 'Yeah, but you just don't know.'

I had my gun out, both bullets at the top by the firing pin. Maude crept out across the stones while I peered round the section of roof, ready to fire if I had to. The noise was coming from a little outhouse a short distance away. Maude tripped on the rubble, and the baby heard her and started to cry again.

She reached the door to the outhouse. She opened it just a tiny fraction. The baby wailed louder, just like a baby. Inside was dark. Maude opened it a bit more, stepped inside, and then it blew up.

I think I might have screamed. I cowered down and hid my face as stones and stuff rained all around me. When it was over, I peered out and the outhouse was still standing but the roof was down and the door had blown right off its hinges. There was no sign of Maude. I turned and I ran. Goddamn me, I ran. I ran out of the farmyard, out of the field beyond it and across the road to where Rowan and the Hamiltons were. They'd been hiding in a rhododendron thicket in this pine plantation, but when I got there, they'd gone. Rowan was still there, crouching down, whimpering.

'Where'd they go?' I asked.

'Not here. It went bang,' he said. Jesus! I must have missed them by moments.

'Why are you here?'

'I wouldn't,' he said. 'I wouldn't go. Wouldn't go, Marti.'

You know? You see? What a brave kid! Three years old and he wouldn't go. How many kids would be like that? As far as he knew, I was never coming back. But he waited anyway, bless him.

I kneeled down and I held him tightly. He was shaking like a leaf. So was I. Then I realised I had to go back. I really did have to go and see, just in case . . . just in case there was anything left, you know? Or if she was just injured? It wasn't a huge bang, but it blew the door off its hinges, I noticed that. And there was a noise that might have been a scream or a groan or something or other when I was running off.

It was so stupid. Such an old trick! A crying baby. They'd done it pretty well. It must have been sound-activated, it was a long recording, and I reckon the baby they recorded was dying. What kind of sicko records a dying baby like that?

But we should have known better. The only thing, when you hear a baby cry it goes right through your spine and into your heart, you know what I mean? Right into your heart, and it bypasses your brain altogether. You just want to help. You can't help it.

Oh, Maude, you were always so smart! Why'd you have to be stupid *then*?

I started to get up, but Rowan flung himself at me. Wrapped his arms around me and pressed his face right into mine.

'Marti, Marti, Marti,' he kept saying. He was panting and gasping at the same time, but he managed to get it out about six or seven times before he closed his eyes tight and started to leak tears.

I knew what the little shit was up to. It was that transparent. He needed me, I was all he had left and he was binding me to him, binding me to him with his baby magic. He was getting his tears all over my face, which was wet anyway. But it worked, you know? If I hadn't already been bound to him, it would have worked anyway.

I held him for awhile, but I was thinking of Maude. I waited for him to calm down a bit.

'You don't need to do that,' I told him. 'You know I love you anyway.'

'Don' go,' he said.

'What about Maudie?' I said. 'I have to see to Maudie, Rowan.'

It took a while to convince him, but in the end he said, ''K.'

So I went to see Maudie.

I really thought I'd heard a voice as I was running away. Maybe it was Maude, maybe I was wrong. I checked the gun. Made sure the bullets were in the right place.

Crept in like a ghost.

She was in there all right, lying on her back in the rubble under the door. That's a sight I'll never forget. Her eyes flicked over to me when I came in.

'You came back,' she whispered.

'Course I came back.'

'That was stupid.'

'Seems to be the theme for the day.'

She looked at me and I looked at her. She was panting away, trying not to pant too hard as it hurt so much. There was a beam across her pelvis. She wasn't anything like so pretty any more. Some of her insides were on the outside.

She nodded at the gun. 'Two bullets.'

'Yeah.'

'One of them for me.'

I shook my head. 'I can't do that.'

'You have to do it, Marti.'

'That's not sticking together, Maudie.'

'It's not always about sticking together,' she said, and I said, 'Never thought I'd hear you say that.'

Then I looked around the place. 'Hey,' I said, 'look on the wall over there, that looks just like Mum.'

And she turned her head away to look.

*

I got out of there quick and I walked back to the rhododendron thicket where I'd left Rowan, but he wasn't there. I had a panic – a proper panic attack. I thought the Hamiltons maybe came back and took him away, or someone else, and for a while I was running about screaming, which was also pretty stupid. When I'd done running around calling and calling to him, I had a thought, so I went back to where we started and I had another little look, quieter this time. I heard him then, his breathing. He was in the same thicket, he'd barely moved at all. He was just hiding from me, because – well, work it out for yourself. He'd heard the shot. Frankly, I wished I could hide from myself.

I found a log and sat down on it.

'I know you're there, Rowan, I can hear you,' I said. And immediately he held his breath, the little toad.

I waited a bit. I so much didn't want to talk about it. I so much didn't want it to have ever happened. Or think about it or talk about it.

'She was so sick, Rowan,' I said. 'Because she was so badly hurt . . .'

That was as far as I got. I cried. Man, I cried. I cried and cried and cried. I was bawling. All the rotten things that had happened! My mum, my dad, my friends. But losing Maude was the worst of them all because she was supposed to be there for ever. I sat there and put my face in my hands and I cried and I cried. All the tears – for me and for Mum and Dad and for Maude, my lovely Maude, who would never leave me, who put up with me being such a dick, who loved me and loved me until I finally had to love her back. And then she went and got herself killed, the fucking stupid bloody cunting cow.

After a while a pair of little arms came around my neck. And of course that set me off even more. Sitting here in the woods, the two of us, bawling our eyes out. Bawling, bawling, bawling our eyes out.

And that's how we were when they found us.

24

There were three of them, a boy and a girl about my age and an older one who was in charge. They were wearing uniforms with the double red cross on a white background. Bloods. My worst nightmare. It *had* to happen. To make matters worse – to make them as bad as they could possibly be – I had my blue dress on and the daisy DMs. I'd dressed up to tease the Hamilton boy. And make-up. With stubble. Perfect. The only accessory I was missing was my handbag, which was hanging around the neck of the girl. They hadn't bothered searching it so far. Inside was my gun. I couldn't take my eyes off it.

The young ones were so excited at catching someone, it'd've been sweet if they weren't actually evil. The boy kept prodding me with his gun – one of those nasty-looking stubby automatics. American weapons. Both him and the girl kept holding them up to their faces and aiming, like on the cop shows.

'I thought you guys were supposed to be retreating down south,' I said, trying to keep my voice as steady as I could. I was speaking to the older one, on the grounds that he might be the nice one, if such a thing exists with this crowd. He had this matchstick sticking out of the corner of his mouth, which he now slowly reached up for, took out and spat.

'Had to stay up here to help keep the place clear of vermin

for when the boys get here,' he said. And Lo! My wishful hopes of mercy came crashing to the ground.

So they weren't exactly official Bloods, but they were armed by the Bloods. They kept bawling at me. The boy called me a *gay poof wog*.

'That's not factually correct,' I told them.

'Put your hands in the air, bitch. Hands up, or I *will* shoot!' yelled the girl. Just like the movies.

I'd picked Rowan up when they got us – which I wasn't sure was the right thing because I was the one they had those guns trained on – so now I had to put him down again to put my hands up, and of course he started pawing at me to be picked up again. I looked at the older one, the one they called Sarge, and I raised my eyebrows.

'Pick him up,' the older guy said.

'Not while they've got those things on me,' I said.

He looked at me and I looked at him. I had a really nasty feeling I'd seen him before. He walked up and patted me down to make sure I was unarmed, during which it became apparent that my person was not all it seemed – as if it wasn't already apparent. He stood up, smirked, looked me in the eye and nodded a couple of times. What's the next stage of fear that comes after pooing yourself? Whatever it is, that's what I was doing then.

They marched us back to their camp like that, the kids behind me with their guns up by their faces, and me clutching Rowan because otherwise those guys would have been beating me to a pulp. Human shield! But for how long would it work? I was going to get beaten to a pulp sooner or later, that's all

I knew. Or killed. Probably the sooner, the better. They were making all these disgusting comments about me and Rowan. You know how it is, once people decide you're a pervert, they like to think that you're capable of all imaginable perversions, even the ones that genuinely are perverted. The sergeant was walking quietly, whistling through his teeth and smiling weirdly at me whenever I looked back and caught his eye. I was whispering sweet things to Rowan – nursery rhymes, mainly. My mum used to sing me endless nursery rhymes, she knew 'em all. Suddenly I could almost hear her singing those silly songs in her sweet low voice. Isn't it funny how the mind works? Then, of all times!

I know what you're thinking. You're thinking, Oh no! This is the actual worst thing that could possibly happen. That's what I was thinking all right. I was thinking, This is it now, Marti, you've finally been caught and it's a bullet in the head for you – if you're lucky. Yep, that's it – dead. You know? Or maybe the ERAC, which was as good as being dead. I mean, I had so much going on in me they'd want to cure, I might actually break the machine.

You might well be thinking that. But we'd both be wrong. That was just me being uncharacteristically optimistic. I was thinking that all I had to worry about was making sure that Rowan got through this. Maybe I could convince them he was white, and that I was looking after him for some neighbours or something, so he'd get sent off and adopted by some nice white supremacist parents. I was also wondering if actually he was better off dead, but in the end I decided I had no right to act on that, and that I'd just have to hope that one day he might remember me. Because if I had to meet him at some point when he had actually turned into the enemy . . .

'I'd rather be dead,' I said out loud.

'You soon will be,' said one of the kids, taking the chance to stick me in the ribs with his weapon.

'Maybe not as soon as he likes,' said the older one.

'What's that supposed to mean?' I asked.

'You'll find out soon enough,' he said. And Lo! So it came to pass.

They marched us back past the hamlet where Maude fell and a couple of miles past to their camp. It was a proper Army thing. Big camouflaged tents, trucks, Jeeps. Everyone had a nice new gun. They even had some of the big stuff, rocket launchers and the like – you know, like a load of big guns mounted on the back of a vehicle, all pointed up at the sky, but really, they were probably trained on a school or a hospital or something fifty miles away. You could do a lot of damage with that sort of thing. I remember thinking, How much does it cost to set one of those off? A hundred thousand a pop? Two hundred? Who knows?

'What are you guys, Bloods?' I asked, because it all looked new and American and sort of proper, with uniforms and all that, but the soldiers didn't act right. The kids with their guns in my ribs didn't know how to take an order. We walked past a field with people training in it, and some of them were so bad, I reckon even I could have handled it better than them.

'Affiliates,' said the older guy, the sergeant.

It was just after that that things took a turn for the worse. The kids were about to take us to a stockade where they had other prisoners, but the sergeant waved his gun and said, 'Over there.'

The kids hesitated. 'HQ?' said one of them. 'Is he important?'

'We'll let Major Tom decide that,' said the sergeant. And he gave me the evil eye. And I gave him the scared eye back, because – Major Tom? *The* Major Tom? I'm not talking Bowie here. Because . . . Not *him*. Of all people, not him. Please, please, *please* don't let it be true . . .

Then the man himself put any remaining doubt out of my mind, when he came out of his tent.

The thing is, I'd never really known how truthful Maude was being when she told me I'd shot his dick off. She has been known to exaggerate. I'd never got round to asking her what it was she'd kicked into the bushes that day – I was too shy. And it felt stupid. Maybe she was just complaining that I'd shot him in the groin, which would be bad enough. So now I had a chance to check him out and . . . it was hard to say. Last time he had a face full of ugly stubble, but he was clean shaven now, so I couldn't tell if he'd lost any facial hair. He didn't look as muscly, though, and maybe his beer gut had moved a little down to his hips. Difficult to say. But he had a baggy T-shirt on and just then a gust blew it flat against his chest.

Now then. Were those tits, or were they moobs? Again . . . difficult to say. They were only little, not much more than an A cup, I'd say. Mits? Toobs? Either way, it wasn't looking good.

'What d'ya think, Major?' asked the sergeant. 'Without the beard?'

'Could be.'

'How many of them do you get wandering around the place? It *has* to be him,' said the sarge.

Major Tom looked at him, then he looked at me.

'Strip it down,' he said. 'Let's see how it looks.'

The two kids looked at each other – they clearly didn't want to get anywhere near me. But it wasn't their job. This was a dirty job, a nasty job. A *Black* job. Not the sort of job you want white hands to sully themselves with.

No problem. They had a man for the job. Yes, Major Tom still had his personal slave. Sebastian, remember him? He came over now to undress me, complaining away just like he did last time.

'Why's it me has to handle the Blacks all the time? Why me, always *me*?' Etc, etc. Everyone around was watching. I was the entertainment now. But then – miracle! He came up close so his head was blocking anyone's view, glanced at me in the eye for a second, and said, 'Sister.'

I think I may have died for a moment. 'Put the kiddie down, fam,' he murmured. Which I did. He kneeled down at my feet and carefully undid my bootlaces and pulled my DMs off. Then he stood up again. 'Now I'm gonna push you down, OK,' he said quietly. He put his foot out and pushed me over, but not too hard.

'Brother,' I said.

'You have to get through this now,' he said.

'Please,' I said.

'I can't help you now, fam. You have to get through this,' he repeated.

'Take care of Rowan for me. I don't want him to watch it,' I said.

He nodded and then he bent down and pulled my dress off. I didn't resist – what was the point? And then he removed my pants and my bra, which he did gently, so that was good, because if it had been any of those white soldiers, it wouldn't have been like that. But even if they had done that, I don't think I could have hated it any more.

I'd not had my meds, I'd not had enough to eat, I'd been doing far too much exercise. I wanted a nice plump female body and what I had now was a skinny boy's one, with tits. A sort of cross between moobs and boobs, whatever that is. I was a mess. My beard had grown and so had most of my other body hair. I had body hair in places I swear I never used to have. And to crown it all there was Mr Knobby and the Heartbreakers hanging down like some kind of monster hanging out of a big, untidy, ugly crow's nest.

When I was finally naked, the Black man held out his hand to Rowan, who had been watching the whole thing with his mouth open. Christ knows what he thought was going on, but who knows what kids think anyway? They're like a different species.

'Go with the nice man, Rowan. I have some business here,' I said.

'No,' he said.

I closed my eyes. He'd always been so good. Please, Rowan – don't pick *now* to throw a wobbler!

'Rowan, you need to go. It's *dangerous* here,' I said. He paused – I held my breath. But he knew well enough that when I said it was dangerous, it was dangerous. He took Sebastian's hand, and let him lead him away.

There was quite a crowd gathered round now. All through it, Major Tom had been staring at me with his narrow beady little eyes. His face had gone as white as a pint of milk. Now he began to walk towards me, eyes fixed on me like gimlets.

I didn't look at him. I ignored him as he closed in. I watched Rowan instead, and when he turned to look, I gave him a cheeky smile and a little wave. Then Sebastian pushed his face into his shoulder. Major Tom was bending down, looking into my face, but I still didn't look back.

Then he started on me.

It was just me and him for maybe five minutes? Who knows? I wasn't counting. Five minutes that changed my life. Not a word was said throughout, like we had some kind of a pact together. I remember the crowd cheering and wincing and going, Whoooooah! Ooooohhh . . . when it was something particularly sadistic or nasty. No details.

When he'd done, they picked me up and carried me, or what was left of me, to a container, a lorry container. They flung me in there with a crowd of other prisoners and an overflowing bucket and banged the door shut.

And that was me, folks. It was dark, pitch dark, in there. The others had to feel out where I was hurt, and bathe me with a little water, which was all the medicine they had.

And that was my home for the next couple of months.

25

Yes, that was my home, me and forty to fifty other people all packed into that container with one bucket and nothing else. We didn't have the whole of the container either. It was divided in two. Our part, the prison part, the Tank we called it, was maybe two thirds of it, and the other part, divided off by a steel wall, was the torture chamber. Several times a day, they would take someone out, always announcing it with an electronic tone, for some reason. *Bing, bong,* you know? Like an electric doorbell. Then you'd hear the bolts and the padlock being undone, the door in the steel wall would open, letting in a flood of light, which was the only light which ever got into the Tank. And each one of us would be praying it'd be someone else and not us. And the soldiers would walk in and one of us would go out with them for 'treatment', as they liked to call it.

You could hear everything. The screams, the confessions. The blaming other people. The begging to do this to someone else, *Not me, not me, no, no, no, please stop, anything, not me. Her in there, behind the wall, they know what you want, they'll say what you need them to. Not me, not me.*

I know what you're thinking. You're thinking, Oooh, now come the gory details. The juicy bits. What did they do to her? Was it rods or whips or sticks or cattle prods, or just boots?

Fire? Electricity, perhaps? What devices? The thumb screws, the strappado? Did they hang her up by her elbows tied behind her back? Did they use spiky things inside?

Forget it. That kind of stuff is private. The tortured never forget. It lives in our minds every day, why would you want it in yours? It's always there, waiting for you. It comes to you unexpectedly, in your sleep, when you walk down the road, while you eat, when you make love. Such memories know no mercy, just as it was when your torturer was working on you. Sounds or smells or sights can set you off – it comes at you out of the blue. It breaks your body and your mind and your feelings and your emotions all over again, every time. You lose everything. It's intimate. I truly expect my torturer's face to be the last face I remember at the end of my days. How could I forget him, and the betrayals he pulled out of me, one by one, like the nails from my fingers?

I hope, I truly hope never to see my comrades from the torture chamber again. And yet how can I ever forget the way we cared for each other when they flung us back to the other side? We touched each other very gently. We forgave every betrayal. Tried to wash the blood and dirt off each other and held hands while we cried.

Each of us was taken out for torture maybe three times a week, maybe twice, maybe four times. One of us was taken out every day for her first week. I think they only stopped because they thought she might die. She was never asked any questions because it wasn't what she *knew* that offended them. It was what she *was*. They made her say filthy things about her mother, her father, her brother, her friends, all the things she loved.

Such memories become a part of you, a big part, perhaps the biggest part. Bigger than your friends, bigger than your lovers, bigger than your childhood, bigger than anything you can know.

So, hearing that, maybe you think you know me now. You'd be wrong. There's nothing I don't want you to know written down here, so don't begin to imagine you know me. My name, perhaps? You think you know that? You think I'm called Marti, or Martina or Martin? You don't know my name. I never lie – *never* – but most of who I am is simply untold. What I choose to tell you is the limit of your rights, and what happened to me in that container – guess, guess, guess away! I won't say. Mostly, it's a secret even from me.

But you do know this much: I got out.

26

Yes, I got out. And for your information not because someone gave me a gun, and not because I took one from the guards and blasted my way out. Little Rowan never found a way to sneak a gun or a knife into the Tank – do me a favour, he was only three! Maude didn't turn out to be alive after all. It wasn't Tariq, who was still in Huntingdon I suppose, or my dad.

But it *was* the cavalry. Far, far, far too late.

The first us prisoners knew of it was the shelling. Massive explosions all around us. The container was shaking from side to side, we were all quaking in terror that we'd get hit – why, I don't know, all of us just wanted to die by then. Then gunfire. Strafing. Mortars. It went on for . . . I don't know how long it went on for. You lose track of time in there. Half a day, I suppose. A day, maybe. Then things quietened down for a while, a good while. Then gunfire again. Then voices. People talking street. American voices. Pakistani voices, South London, Manc, Scouse. It was like the United Nations out there.

We waited quietly, still scared to speak out. Finally, one of us, I forget who, starting banging on the container. Our guards, who were next door in the torture chamber, started hissing at us to shut up, but it was already too late for them.

Then the sudden clatter as they opened the door, which was in the other compartment. Shouts.

The torturers . . . 'Thank God you came,' they said. Trying to make out they were the victims, the lying bastards. But we yelled and when our rescuers opened our door, the real door, they knew in an instant.

'What's going on here?'

'Man, it's minging!'

'It stinks!'

And daylight, suddenly in our eyes. The breeze from outside.

It was a strange coalition who had rescued us: the New English Army, although they weren't all English. It had been formed when British Black and Asian soldiers, sailors and aircrew took up arms against the Bloods. They helped train up other people of colour and teamed up with some Black US troops who were stranded over here when the dollar fell and had been having the same trouble with their own army. It was a separatist group – they wanted a land of their own for our people. It didn't have to be big, but it had to be Black, Black, Black. I wasn't sure about that myself. They kept telling me I was Black, but I had a white mum, didn't I? I have white family over in Ireland, who treated me kindly years ago before things got to this. So where did that leave me?

And Rowan, who's as pale as a plate of pasta?

'Black,' they said, without even having seen him. Just one drop of Black blood made you Black, according to the NEA. I figured they were going to need more land than they knew to house all those white Black people.

I know what you're thinking. You're thinking, Rowan? Yes, what happened to him? I was asking as soon as my mind began to tick – suddenly, in the middle of eating some rice. But Rowan wasn't there.

Sebastian hadn't kept him close at all. To be fair, as a slave, he didn't have much option. He found someone else to care for him, though. A group of working girls had set up camp on the edge of the site – two caravans, one for living in, one for working in – and he'd given Rowan to them to look after. Which was fine, except that a few days before the shelling started, the girls struck camp and moved on, and they'd taken Rowan with them.

I was – not angry. I was too broken to be angry. But bitter and disappointed. I turned my head away and refused to look at him when he came to visit me.

'Jesus, man! What was I supposed to do? Walk round with him on my hip all day while I'm pretending to be their houseboy?' he hissed. But I wouldn't answer. I just made up my mind that as soon as I could walk again, I was going after him – as soon as!

Sebastian came back the next day and told me there was a search going on, but I still wouldn't speak to him. But he was back the next day, and the next.

I raised my eyebrows at him – like, You still here?

'Yes, I'm still here. You the . . . person who shot Major Tom's dick off. You're my hero.'

There was that little pause before 'person'. But I was willing to give that a miss for now. And that was it – we were friends. I was still angry but really, he'd done his best for me – and here he still was. He'd joined up with the NEA and he was doing his best to find those prossies and get my brother back. Which wasn't going to be that easy. The NEA called themselves an army, but there weren't that many of them – just this bunch and a few scouts out there, looking about for Blood-funded militias to take out. They were over the moon having taken out this lot, because they'd captured all those rocket launchers and other weaponry. Now they were sitting still for a while, learning how to use their new toys.

Me and Sebastian got on well together, as it happens. Really, I could forgive him anything after he'd said 'Sister' to me when he had to undress me.

And he would have done anything for me. That thing I said to him about what was his favourite food his mother cooked for him, that was what started him off finding himself hidden away behind all that Blood rewriting they'd done. Me asking that made his mouth water, see, but he had no memory at all what his mouth was watering at. So he was going around for a couple of days wondering about it, about why he couldn't remember what food it was, and then, *hey*, why didn't he remember his mother all that well, either, although he felt that he loved her? And then, Lo! Someone on the camp cooked the very self-same thing that his mother used to. Rice pudding. So he smelled that – like my dad said, you see? Smells! – and then the memories started to come back to him.

'I started to dribble at the thought of that rice,' he told me. 'And I was ready to go and get some – it was *mine*, that's how I felt. I was annoyed that someone had stolen *my* rice pudding. But when I knocked at the door and asked for some, I got chased away. So I went away and I wept, Marti, I just wept.

And in the morning when I got up, I remembered my mother again.'

And he remembered a little more day by day, and finally he realised what was actually going on. So he ran away. And they chased him and caught him and whipped him, like they whip a slave. So he had to stay, and he had to pretend he still thought he was a white man, which was hard, because he kept switching from one personality to the other with no control, and he was terrified that Major Tom and the others would spot it and send him back to the ERAC to be reconditioned.

Yes, it's a crazy world, brothers and sisters. Sebastian had resurrected his good old self, but the bad Blood self was still in there, too, with a crazy set of memories about how the white people had looked after him so well, and let him eat their leftovers, which was too good for him, really, because he was a *savage* with *savage* tastes that could never appreciate good food like a white person could. And how the white people had civilised the Black folk but the Black folk hadn't learned how to be grateful etc, etc.

Sometimes, he'd start talking fondly about his days with 'the guys', and it'd turn out he was talking about his captors, and I'd have to say, 'Ah, the good old days, when you got whipped for running away from home because they didn't share their rice pudding with you.' And he'd shake his head and scowl at me, and then he'd stalk away to try and get his head together again.

Also, he had a whole set of responses that weren't his – like the time I started talking about Malcolm X and he went, 'That no-good negro,' just like that. And you should have seen the look on his face! Surprised isn't the word.

'I never said that,' he said.

'I think you just did,' I said. I knew what was going on, even if he didn't. Poor old Seb was programmed with one of the really early versions of the Blood rewriting software. My dad had been working on number three, but Seb was full of number one, which was read-only. So whenever he said anything that was good and strong and Black, he had some stupid response wired through.

It drove him crazy. 'It's like living with a racist in my head,' he groaned.

But I told him he'd be OK once he got the microchip taken out. He had no idea it was there, even, but I found it for him, tucked in under a little roll of fat at the top of his neck. He couldn't believe it. He must have been programmed never to touch it. It would have been nice to think he might get the chip blocked if my dad's software worked, but like I say, version one was read-only. He had to have it taken out and nothing else would do. Which was easier said than done, because it could go off with a bang – they wired those things to explode if you messed with them. So poor old Seb had to wait.

And his real name, his real Black name *was* Sebastian! How about that? He was adopted by white parents, both doctors in Sussex. He was a nice, white, middle-class boy, and he'd *always* spoken with a nice, white middle-class accent too. But the odd thing was, after his rewriting and then coming back to himself, he always spoke in a Brixton, south London accent ever after – as long as I knew him, anyway.

I asked him what age he was adopted.

'Age four,' he said. So I guess that sorted out where he'd spent his first four years, anyhow.

The NEA had put us ex-prisoners in various huts and tents while we recovered. I was in the officer's dorm with four other people from the Tank. All men. I guess my bits confused them, they often do, but I didn't have the heart to complain.

It was strange. We'd lived together in that hell for so long. We'd all been broken, we'd betrayed everything we knew and loved, including each other. Suddenly here we were in a new life. Gradually we got to know one another better and . . .

Frankly, it was embarrassing. I suppose you want me to talk about the bond between us, how we'd been through so much and come out the other end closer. You might expect it. All we had in that place was each other and we looked after each other so well while we were in there. We really did. But outside, it wasn't like that. One by one we got better, and people began to leave. Sometimes they came back to visit, but always as a duty rather than a need to be together again. Because – why would you? Torture is something you never get over. You don't even ever get to learn to live with it. Why would anyone want to be reminded of it even more than they already are?

Funny thing is, I think about them every day, my container comrades. Sometimes I think I may even love them. But I was happy to see them go away and none of us have made any effort to get in touch. I wonder how they're doing, if they've got on with their lives, how much it changed them, how many were just broken, how many have made lives worth living. I'm curious, I admit it. And yet, if there was ever a reunion, I wouldn't go. None of the others would either, I bet. It would be the strangest reunion in the world – a room full of love, with no one in it. Once, I had dreams of being a pretty girl, but the container put paid to that. My nose was halfway across my face, my jaw was crooked, my shoulder had been dislocated so often I couldn't lift it above my chest. My ribs were cracked. I limped. One eye was cloudy. I'd lost most of my teeth. Just about the only thing I had from my past was my handbag. Yes, that was the only constant companion I kept throughout the whole journey. Sebastian got his hands on it somehow and kept it for me while I was in the Tank. Somehow, he even kept my gun.

'Why on Earth didn't you use it?' I asked him.

'With one bullet in it? You crazy, girl!'

I was in the hospital dorm for a month and all I wanted to do was get on my feet and go find my brother. Easier said than done. I was weak – so, so weak. They'd broken my feet and toes, which healed like crabs, so I've never been able to do much more than hobble ever after. Still, at least I could walk. Slowly, slowly, I got better – road-ready, as Sebastian called it. Bit by little bit.

So the journey goes on, but before I take you out on the road with me again, I have a few things that happened to tell you.

First is this. That software I took down south? It worked! What do you think of that? Can you imagine? I told you my dad was a clever man. Maybe he was even a genius, because he worked out how to do it months ago, and everyone else had all that extra time to work on it but it was still his software that did the trick. Yeah, the NEA had the news – there'd been a breakout from the ERAC. Hundreds, maybe thousands of people got their lives back, their memories, themselves, and they broke out and went running for freedom.

How about that? All down to my dad. And me – and Maude. I cried when I heard that because it meant she hadn't died for nothing.

'You did it, Maude,' I said. Because it was her, it was all her, really. If it had been left up to me, I'd have been sitting on that phone as my own personal tunes repository to this day, and never even worried about all those people.

And . . . what about my dad? According to the NEA, a lot of people got recaptured and put back in. Was he one of them? Or maybe he was sitting with Tariq in a bar somewhere, downing a bottle of wine. Or on the run, or . . .

Who knows? I had business in Amsterdam, I couldn't go back down there without some sort of clue. But . . . there was hope. Last time I had hope about my dad, it nearly killed me. This time, after all I'd been through, I just let it sit. I'd find out about him one day. Or not.

Another thing I want to tell you about is Judgment Day for Major Tom. It was only a week or two after our release. They took me out into the field behind the hospital. I was still so weak, they had to push me in a wheelchair. There was quite a crowd come to watch.

Major Tom was there. So were the torturers. *My* torturer. I won't tell you his name, because as far as I'm concerned he has no name. Him and Major Tom and a few others, standing with their hands tied behind their backs. And behind them, a big deep hole.

Well, we knew what that hole was and so did they. Major Tom was in a mess, weeping under his gag. Some kind of begging, I suppose. My torturer was standing next to him, and it was like he couldn't quite get his head around what was going on. He kept turning to stare at Major Tom, and then look at us as we all trooped in, and then back at the hole behind him. I have no idea what was going through his head. He must have expected something like this. I have this feeling he couldn't get it into his head that it was going to be public, for some reason. All the pain he ever dealt with was done in private.

I don't know what I think about it now. Some of the other people from the Tank wanted to do it themselves, to be the one who pulled the trigger.

'I want to look into his eyes while I blow his f*****g brains out,' someone said. The NEA didn't allow it, they wanted it to be official. Me, I didn't really even want to watch. I wasn't going to, until Sebastian told me I needed to be a witness, which convinced me at the time. It seemed important somehow. These days, I'm not sure. If I had the time again, I doubt I'd go. It was a mistake. Whenever I remember it, watching that man standing there waiting to die, the bile rises up into my mouth and I'm so full of hatred and fear, I can feel my blood curdling in my veins.

When the time came, when the firing squad came out and the order to take aim was called, Major Tom shook his head violently. *Bang!*

My torturer didn't beg. He nodded, as if this was what he

expected or deserved or something. Or as if he was giving permission.

BANG.

Yes, I can be so full of hatred, but there is one thing and one thing only that stops me from ever being the truly bitter and twisted bitch I should have become. I was never the same again after I was tortured. That man changed me, he changed me more than you will ever know. But he wasn't the first. Maude got there first. She broke her way into my heart and she's still there. It's where she lives. She hasn't let me go, she never will. She's the brave one, she's the loving one, the stick-together one, the kind one. Not me. She's dead now but she lives inside me and nothing anyone can ever do can take that away. We were never lovers, but even so, she is the love of my life. She was never tortured. She was never changed. She never will be changed. She will always be the same – my now and for ever Maude. *My* Maude. She should be alive, not me. But since she's dead, well – I have to be alive for her.

The other thing is – I got Rowan back! Yes, they found him for me. It took ages to locate him, during which time I was imagining all sorts of horrors – you can imagine after what happened to Malcom. For a bit, it looked as though I'd lost him for good, because the girls were heading south to try and join up with the Bloods. But being ladies of business, they'd paused to make a few bucks at an FNA camp for a while, and our fellas caught up with them there.

When Rowan came back, I was afraid he wouldn't recognise me after what had been done to me. And he *was* scared at first. He came up to me very slowly as I lay on the bed. Step by step . . .

I said, 'Rowan,' a few times – I didn't have my old voice, but I'd been practising. He came to stand by the bed and looked at me, just stood there, looking. I let him. He looked me all over – at my face, at my hands and feet, at my legs. He came close. He stroked my face. Then he climbed on top of me and lay there saying, 'Marti, Marti, Marti,' while I nodded and hugged him back hard.

So that was us together again. Brother and sister.

And there you are. And was I happy. The changed Marti? Changed by my torturer, changed by Maude, changed by losing everyone except little Rowan?

We all have our demons, don't we? Don't imagine that mine got smaller because I loved Rowan, they didn't, they didn't at all. I was still the same old selfish, greedy, self-serving Marti Okoro that I ever was, still prepared to sell my grandmother for a stale crust – and your grandmother, and you, whoever you are. But Maude had somehow clawed my heart open and a little boy called Rowan crept in. That's all. Perhaps it's a big difference, perhaps it's only a small one, I don't know. All I can say is that the stale crusts I sold your grandmother for are shared between me and him these days.

That's it. I wonder sometimes if Rowan would be better off without me, and if I've done him any favours at all by us sticking together. But here we are. What's done is done, and that's one thing that all the hot knives, the boots and clubs in the world, or all the drugs or the boys or the girls, or wads of cash or jewels (not that I've ever seen any of them!) can't ever undo.

27

We carried on, me and Rowan, one bullet between us, which, please the Lord, I hoped I'd never have to use, heading northeast for Hull and the ferry out of hell.

The Bloods advance had stalled – they'd even had to retreat a bit, but maybe not for long. This was our best chance to make our escape from jolly old England. Trouble was, it was everyone else's chance as well. The roads were fuller than ever. People were trying to get home, or find a new home or escape or whatever. Some were trying to get to Scotland – a lot of Pakistanis, for some reason. Others were trying to go west, to Liverpool and on to Ireland and beyond, to the Caribbean, perhaps. No one wanted to go to America any more, of course. An awful lot of them, same as us, were headed for Hull. If you wanted to get to Europe and on to Pakistan or anywhere in Asia, or south to Africa, Hull was where you started out. We were just two out of hundreds of thousands. And where was our place in that queue?

But Amsterdam was still calling! Somehow I was going to get there, and I truly felt that after all I'd been through, nothing could stop me now. I'd been dreaming about it for so long that I'd started to think of it as home. Maude was dead, Mum was dead. My dad – maybe, maybe not. But for now, Rowan was all I had in the world – and we were going home.

We stuck to the big roads – I'd had enough of criss-crossing the fields and climbing gates. It was different anyway, with no Maude to help me. The boys at the camp had found us a pushchair – not for Rowan though. It carried food, tent, clothes, all our stuff. I needed the smooth roads to push it along. Sometimes Rowan rode on top of the stuff, but mostly he had to walk – there was no way I could carry him, those whores had spoiled the little swine, he was an absolute piglet. I thought he'd slow us down, but while he'd been stuffing his face, I'd been getting my kidneys liquidised with a big stick, and it was me who had to call a halt first. My feet! They hurt so much. I did toughen up a bit and by the time we got to Hull I was up to seven or eight miles a day, but even then, I was wiped out the day after.

Not much happened apart from walking. The war had stalled behind us. The charities and NGOs were free to come in and help us, businesses were still functioning. The shops were open – some, anyway. I bought Rowan a second-hand console so he could play games. Got myself a new phone, downloaded my numbers and my tunes. Had some chats with Sebastian and some of the folk from the NEA – I'd made some friends there. Chatted to a few mates. Tried to call my dad and my brothers; no reply.

And we walked and we walked and we walked. And in the end, we made it – yeah! Several months late, but when was I ever on time? Hull! Ferries! Escape! Amsterdam! Sex, drugs and rock 'n' roll.

Er, excuse me? Did I say sex? Forget it. Look at the state of me. Did I say rock 'n' roll? We had no money, I'd spent the lot.

Did I say Amsterdam and escape? We joined a long, long queue of refugees waiting for some charity or other to get us out of there – hundreds of thousands of us living in shanty towns, squatting on the beaches, sleeping in the parks. Most of us were in these enormous camps that had been set up in industrial lots and old warehouses outside town. Park and Stay. No charge.

No one likes a refugee. Getting a ticket for the ferry was hard, and that wasn't the end of it. You needed a passport, a job waiting for you over there, a visa, papers for this, papers for that. All those things cost money. A better bet was to get yourself smuggled across the sea in a small boat – a fishing boat if you were lucky, an inflatable dinghy if you weren't. None of them were all that cheap either.

We spent a few weeks living in one of the camps on the edge of town. My money was at an end and it wasn't long before things started to look a bit desperate. There was some cash around, grants and loans and stuff, mainly from the EU. You could get money to start a business if you had some skills. But what skills did I have? None. Accidentally shooting dicks off racists wasn't on the approved list. The charities were there, thank God. They'd all been preparing to pack up and leave when they thought the Bloods were on their way, but that hadn't happened, so here they still were, for now, anyway.

No one knew for sure what was going on further south. There were all sorts of rumours going round about how well the rebels were doing, how much funding they had, how many arms, what kinds of arms. China was supporting them! . . . Er, no, hang on, no, not China, it was the EU sending in the warplanes and gunships. Or the Saudis . . . ? Plenty of people were happy to think that the tide had turned, that the Bloods were on the run. As far as I was concerned, things could change at any time. The charities would up sticks and make a run for it, and then what? I'd just had a taste of the Bloods, or something like them. I didn't fancy getting a second dose of that, thanks a lot.

One thing I knew and one thing only – there was plenty of shit about and there were plenty of fans about; pretty soon, one was going to hit the other. We needed to get out. But how? If Maude had been alive, she'd've kept all three of us going by teaching, or . . . who knows what? I never got to the end of her skills, never found the beginning of mine, either.

Like everyone else, I kept going into Hull from the camp to try and find work in the city, but what could I do? I can't walk properly, I can't even talk properly any more. I have no skills. I'm as ugly as a handful of rubble. I did my best to keep a happy-looking face on the front of my head for Rowan's sake, but I can tell you, if it hadn't been for him, I would have ended it all. What did I have to live for? All my dreams had been taken from me. I had literally nothing going for me.

And then came the most unlikely piece of luck I ever had in my life. It came in the form of a great, big, dirty-arsed sailor, who'd fought his way across from Liverpool to try and get a boat from Hull, and failed. He was sitting on his hairy backside outside a minging little bar on Oxbow Street.

'Ten,' he slurred as I walked past.

'Ten what?' I said.

'Ten *pouns*,' he said.

I was looking round, wondering what he was on about and if he was talking to me.

'What for?'

'A shag. Or a blow job,' he told me, and he gave me a lopsided grin.

I was deeply offended – not because he was offering to pay me for sex, but because it was obviously a joke. Who was going to pay to sleep with me? Look at me! Hairy, broken and ugly. I was always pretty ugly to start with, but now I was the Queen of Ugly. My nose was broken, my jaw twisted sideways, I had feet like crabs. I'd lost half my teeth, my face was smashed. I hadn't seen a med for months. I'd grown scrawny boy muscles in odd places, all twisted by my limp. My tits had grown sideways and floppy. The only identity I had left was my blue dress and my make-up, and even though it was dangerous walking around dressed like that, it was all I had so I did it anyway.

I ignored him and walked on, shaking my head.

'OK, fifteen,' he said. 'It's all I have. Honest.'

I turned back to look. He actually sounded serious. Could it really be . . . ?

'Twenty,' I told him. And he grumbled and said he could have got a proper woman for that – which really *was* offensive! – but this was business. So I did it. He had a little shanty tucked away, more of a dog kennel, really. I had to wipe him down from head to foot with a wet rag before we got down to it, and he lay on his bed, grinning up at me because I was going to be the first sex he'd had for a month. Twenty pounds! I mean, it's nothing, but I went home feeling rich, and Rowan and I ate proper food that night. A few days later I went back to see him – John his name was – to see if he wanted a repeat performance. He did, but he had no money left – just a fiver, enough for a meal and not much else.

'Food before sex,' he said, regretfully. But he did offer to put me in touch with some friends. So we shared that five-pound meal and I stayed the night in the kennel, and he was as good as his word. He was a nice guy, John, just such an alky.

People look down on sex workers. It's a job, same as other jobs. And you know what? It seemed like a natural progression. The final item on the list of undesirable things that was Marti Okoro. What a transformation, eh? All the way from iron virgin to hooker in the space of a few months.

I was the cheapest girl on the street, but it paid the bills. I wore the boots, found myself a new dress, wore my hair long, smeared on some lippy across my gob, and finished it off with too much blusher. I'd been doing my best to find meds at every stop along the way but there was nothing. Maybe it was too late for that anyhow. Regardless, I made a living for me and for Rowan.

I nearly got into trouble for it. After I started hanging around the dank streets in the poor quarters, a couple of working women came along.

'You're working our patch,' one of them said – very aggressive.

Which was true. But when they saw how I was close up, they decided I was catering for a very particular clientele and let me alone. And Lo! It came to pass that Marti Okoro found herself work, which is no shame on anyone. I got beat up from time to time, but then that was always something I had to put up with. We ate . . . we kept warm . . . we wore clothes . . . and I even managed to put a little bit away every day.

And finally the day came when the Lord smiled down on poor Marti and all the many sins she had committed for to keep her little brother Rowan innocent, in the form of a big fat old white man with a taste for the unusual . . .

He gave me a hard time, that guy – wanted a lot for his twenty pounds. I got punched, I got choked, I got kicked. I was on my knees on the hard floor for ages, but when we'd done, he fell asleep in a drunken stupor on the bed and started snoring like a pig with a bad cold. Which gave me the chance to riffle through his pockets for his wallet. And I found his wallet. And Lo! It was fat, fat, fat.

I sat there a while, wondering what to do. Was I tempted? What do you think? Was I scared? You bet. There were a lot of people milling around Hull at that time, but even so, if anyone put out the word that they wanted to find the hairy trans hooker with a broken face, broken teeth and crooked feet, they weren't going to have to look hard. I admit it, right here, that this wasn't the first punter whose pockets I'd been through. Nice guys as well as nasty, there's no honour among thieves, you must know that by now. But so far I hadn't taken one single penny – not out of the strictness of my moral code, in case you've managed to read this far without learning a thing about me. No. It was the fear of retribution and ruining my business model.

There was only one theft I could ever make, and that was the big one. The fat one. The one that would give me and Rowan enough money to get on the boat and away, away, away to Amsterdam, city of sex, drugs, safety, food, housing and education.

How much did I need for that? I needed a thousand pounds. Five hundred a head. More than I could earn in a month of

Sundays. And how much did Mr Slapsie have in his wallet? Three hundred US dollars.

There was a time when dollars were almost as cheap as toilet paper, but it'd been a long, long time since you could get a pound for under two of them. I wasn't sure of the amount I had in my hands as I sat there on the edge of the bed, but I was fairly sure that I was still a good few pounds down on the price for two places in Simon the boatie's dinghy, which was the cheapest way that I knew of to get across the water (if you were lucky).

Simon's prices were rock bottom because of the dinghy, but the fact was, he was still in business after ten trips, despite high seas and a small flotilla of EU cruisers attempting to intercept him getting across. So he had to be doing something right. But – he was rock solid on his price. Five hundred a head. That's what you paid – in full, no bargaining, cash up front before you got on the boat.

But this was dollars. People preferred dollars to pounds, because the pound was up and down like my mood swings, whereas the dollar was fast rising up the desirable currency lists once again. Maybe, just maybe, it would be possible to bargain with him with the dollars, plus the bit I had saved back in my tent, buried two feet down under my bedding in the wet Hull clay.

Tricky call. So what did I do? Hey – you must know me by now. Take a guess.

So here we are. Here we are, on the water's edge, in a big fat inflatable on a sea that is as still and as smooth as I've ever seen.

The big round old moon spilling silver all around us. What could possibly go wrong? Simon the boatie is as sober as I can remember seeing him. We all know that his wife ran off with their child a few months ago and that he's well known for his frequent drunken claims in the dockside bars that he has nothing left to live for. He has been known to put to sea in a storm, more or less.

Yes, the gods of weather and chance are smiling on us tonight. True, the dinghy is a little overcrowded, but what do you expect? This is business.

'You said there'd only be twelve people onboard,' complains a young man, who ought to know better. Next to him, the love of his life hugs her baby and looks anxiously at Simon the boatie.

'You pays your money, you takes your chance,' Simon says. 'Anyone want out, get out now, while we're still on the beach. No refunds.'

The faces of the young couple look so, so white in the pale moonlight. The man looks anxiously at big John, who accompanies Simon on these trips. John extends a generous hand to the beach.

Pause. The young couple look at each other and shake their heads. They're staying. Who can blame them? Setting off from an uncertain land on an uncertain sea towards an uncertain welcome. But one thing when you're a refugee: you get used to being on the move.

John gets out, pushes the dinghy off the pebbles and . . . we're off! We're away. Off to Amsterdam, land of . . . well. You must know by now.

*

Do you want to know a secret? One of the dark and nasty things I've done that has been glossed over in this record, if not baldly lied about? I expect you do, but whether you do or not, I'm going to give it to you anyway, just to show you that whatever else, I'm still the old Marti, here in my heart. Just because my heart now beats for Rowan as well as myself, doesn't make me any nicer or more likeable.

You know that nasty piece of work whose dollars had paid for our passage on the dinghy? The fat old white man, who was even now wandering the streets of Hull without a penny to his name, wondering where that ugly but obliging hooker disappeared with all his money? Yeah, well, he wasn't nasty at all. He was actually a rather nice old gentleman. All he wanted was for me to lie down with him and stroke his face and murmur sweet nothings in his ear before we had perfectly ordinary sex. But I stole his money anyway, because that's the kind of girl I am – the kind of girl who will do anything, anything at all, no matter how scummy or nasty, to look after me and mine. I'm just the same as I always was. It's just, like I say, that my heart now beats for two, not one.

Why am I telling you this? Maybe because it's the last thing I'm going to tell you, ever, and although I don't want you to know everything about me, or even a lot about me, at the same time I don't want you to leave with any illusions.

At least, I think that might be it, but it might not be. It might also be because of what happened next. Which is, that karma came to get me. It was a funny sort of karma, which had no sense of justice or good or bad, no moral code or anything like that. Just a sense of irony, perhaps. Or sarcasm. Maybe that's it. In the face of the sarcastic Fates, I want you to know that I'm still a bitch, no matter what.

What happened is this: my phone went off. On vibrate, we were trying to be quiet and I'm not that stupid. I took it out and looked at it, and on the screen it said . . . You'll never guess. Or will you? Unbelievably, incredibly, given the timing . . . it was my dad. My fucking cunting bloody dad.

'Marti,' he went. 'You're still alive! Marti, my darling, my darling, *darling* daughter.'

'You bastard!' I yelled. 'You fucking bastard! How dare you! How fucking dare you – *now*? Now, you bastard? Now!'

'Hey, Marti,' he said, and he gave that chuckle he has when he's anxious and trying to reassure you at the same time. 'Marti! You OK, girl?'

Everyone on the boat was hissing at me like a basketful of snakes, because, I mean, while no one was that bothered about boats leaving the shore to cross the cold North Sea, it was still a secret kind of activity; and believe me, I was screaming the house down. Big John got up to come and sort me out, but the whole boat wobbled so he had to sit down.

'Shut your f*****g mouth or you're going over the side,' he hissed.

'Marti, you OK?' said my dad again.

'OK. I have a situation to deal with. I'll ring you back,' I said. I put the phone away. And – I wasn't mucking around here – I took the gun out. No messing. There was a collective gasp from my fellow passengers.

'We need to go back to shore,' I said.

Simon shook his head. 'Shoot me dead,' he said.

'No such luck,' I said. I pointed the gun not at him, at Big John.

'Marti?' said Rowan. 'Are we going home?' Home, you remember, for Rowan, being Amsterdam.

'We need to pick up our dad first, baby,' I said.

Simon shrugged and turned his head away, heading out to the open sea. Everyone else in the boat was begging him to turn around. John was staring at me like he meant to murder me, which he probably did. I quietly drew back the firing pin on my gun. One bullet. It had to come in handy one day.

'Turn the boat round,' said John suddenly. Simon glanced back to look at him. 'Turn it round, I said,' snarled John. Simon paused . . . paused some more . . . then turned the boat around.

I kept the gun out for the few minutes it took to get back to the shore. I had no idea if the bullet was in the right place in the chamber or not, but it was enough. John was staring at me like a viper the whole way. I didn't care. On the way, I was thinking about things. All sorts of things went through my head. About the journey, about Maude. About Rowan.

'Are you getting out or aren't you?' asked Big John.

And I said . . .

'No. Change of plan.' I dipped my head. 'Sorry. We're going to Amsterdam.'

It was quite funny, looking back. In fact, it was funny at the time, because every single person in the boat started moaning at me exactly as if I'd just made the taxi home from a shopping expedition go right out of its way to drop me off, and then decided not to get out after all. All of them, at the same time. Bitching away. It made me laugh.

'Sorry,' I said. 'Look, I made a mistake. That phone call. But it's OK now. Let's go.'

So the grumbling died down, and we pushed off again. John had to get his feet wet a second time so I was not the most popular person in the dinghy – but we set off on our way to Amsterdam, City of Sin. I tucked the gun down into my belt, close at hand, just in case I might still need it. One bullet left. It's the great thing about bullets – you don't always have to use them for them to work. I let out a big sigh and pulled Rowan onto my lap and rested my chin on the top of his head. I didn't ring back – we were getting out of range anyway. I'd save that for the other side. Leaving my dad behind was like . . .

But you know what? I've had enough now, explaining everything that happens to the likes of you. So tell you what – why don't you work it out for yourself? You've heard enough about me – all you ever will hear, that's for sure. If you can't work it out now, you never will. Enough to say that the cold North Sea slapped against the prow of the dinghy, like a hungry cat playing with a tiny mousey as we sailed off into the unknown. I held Rowan tight and prayed to my own private, nonexistent gods to carry us safely to the other side. And I thought to myself, how odd life is, that you can end up doing exactly the same thing for two entirely different reasons.

My name is Martina Okoro. I don't know much, but what I do know is whose side I'm on. I'm on Rowan's side. I'm on Dad's side and Tariq's side. I'm on the side of the NEA and the FNA and one day, when I have the time, I'm going to come back and fight for what's mine. This England belongs to me and to people like me. One day I'll be back, and when I am, it won't be just three bullets I'll be having. I'll be armed to the teeth. Just watch me.

Acknowledgements

My partners in crime, Pete Kalu and Tariq Mehmood, have been incredibly generous with their time and efforts, reading through the drafts, putting me right and advising me on matters of race, ethnicity, politics, philosophy, all things literature and much else beside. Thanks, boys! It's been a real pleasure.

Thanks also to Jenet le Lacheur for reading through the book and helping me out on trans issues so well. Special thanks are due to Kim Blackburn, Quen Took and Beck Simpson for providing so much passion, enthusiasm and commitment into the project. You really helped give me faith in this book.

To Muli Ameye for help on getting Marti's mixed heritage right and to Lucy Christopher for her notes, special thanks are due.

In Italy, thanks to Pepe Bianco and Davide Pace for looking after me and helping me organise and carry out my interviews. And special thanks to George, to Mervat and to Hisham and his family for telling me their stories, and what it's like to live in a war zone.

Thanks to Eloise Wilson for the final spit and polish, to Chloe Sackur for her efforts on the book's behalf. And last but not least, my editor Charlie Sheppard, who takes no prisoners in making sure that the book is the best I and she can make it. Charlie, your name ought to be on the front somewhere. Thanks a million.

JUNK

25TH ANNIVERSARY EDITION

MELVIN BURGESS

WINNER OF THE CARNEGIE MEDAL AND THE GUARDIAN CHILDREN'S FICTION PRIZE

With an introduction by Malorie Blackman

Tar loves Gemma, but Gemma doesn't want to be tied down – not to anyone or anything. Gemma wants to fly. But no one can fly forever. One day, somehow, finally, you have to come down.

Junk is a powerful novel about a group of teenagers caught in the grip of heroin addiction. Once you take a hit, you will never be the same again.

'Everyone should read *Junk*'
The Times

'Ground-breaking . . . remains the best book about teenagers and drugs to this day'
Guardian

The Lost Witch

MELVIN BURGESS

Bea has started to hear and see things that no one else can – creatures, voices, visions. Then strangers visit Bea and tell her she is different: she has the rare powers of a witch. They warn her she is being hunted. Her parents think she is hallucinating and needs help. All Bea wants to do is get on with her life, and to get closer to Lars, the mysterious young man she has met at the skate park. But her life is in danger, and she must break free. The question is – who can she trust?

'Extraordinary'
Simon Mayo,
Simon Mayo's Books of the Year podcast

'Rich, twisty storytelling'
Sunday Times